John Durham

from The Clarks

1957

OUTCAST, STALLION OF HAWAII

OUTCAST

Stallion of Hawaii

by

HARLAN THOMPSON

Doubleday & Company, Inc.
Garden City, New York
1957

ACKNOWLEDGMENT The author wishes to make grateful acknowledgment to Gwen and Roger Williams for their hospitality and help in gathering material for this book while a guest at Kukaiau Ranch. Thanks also to Theo H. Davies & Co., Ltd., for permission to use the Kukaiau Ranch name, and similarly to various members of the ranch: Frank Correia, foreman, John Holi Mae, Danny, and others. Finally, special thanks to Edwin H. Bryan, Jr., Curator of Collections, and the staff of the Bernice P. Bishop Museum, Honolulu, and to Homer Hayes, newspaperman, resident of the "Big" Island and noted authority on Hawaiian lore, for their help in supplying material on the mores and customs of Hawaii, past and present.

This book, while of factual background and locale, is entirely fictional.

To Harlan Holt with love

CONTENTS

OUTCAST, STALLION OF HAWAII

Chapter 1

FASTEN YOUR SEAT BELT

•

Bart Holiday got a fleeting glimpse of a little half-moon bay fringed with ragged palm trees as the DC-3 plane circled for a landing.

"That's Kailua, where they used to load cattle for Honolulu," said Homer Kanoa, in his low Hawaiian voice.

The lighted sign flashed on, "Fasten Your Seat Belt," and Bart began to fumble with his.

The plane righted itself and moved gracefully for a landing. Through the opposite window Bart caught sight of the same half-moon bay, then the grass shacks around Queen Liliuokalani's summer palace of long ago, on whose lawn they still held festive feasts, or *luaus* as they were known on the islands.

"It looks just like Doc said it would," Bart replied. "You know Doc was a veterinarian here on the Big Island for years. That's how he got to know the Hunters and the Kukaiau ranch."

Bart's mind swung back to Doc Holiday's little animal hospital in Lincoln, Nebraska, on the day that significant letter had arrived from Dick Hunter six months ago. The letter telling that the Hunters' son Des had been killed by a fall from a horse. The cow pony had hit a thin place above a lava tube and gone down.

"It seems Des was killed instantly—neck broken," Doc had explained to Bart who'd just come in from the kennels.

"That's tough," Bart had said.

"Right," Doc had replied.

What else could you say when you heard that kind of news about a Des Hunter, who was young, well-loved, and part of the future of a great cattle ranch?

Then a second letter had come. Doc had called Bart in from the kennels and made him sit down in a chair opposite him, as he'd done as far back as Bart could remember.

"The Hunters are lonely," Doc had said directly. "They've got their daughter Anastasia, who's fourteen, but they're feeling the loss of Des. I wrote them about you." He paused to let the words sink in.

Bart had started to get out of his chair. He was quick. He got the idea.

"No, sir," he declared. "I like it here with you."

Doc had just grinned. "Sure you do. But with fifty thousand acres of land and six thousand head of cattle needing a boss some day, and with the Hunters offering you a wonderful home and this chance, what do you say?"

Bart began to see he had no choice. He couldn't let Doc down by refusing to go. Dr. Lawrence P. Holiday, who had found him on the doorstep in a wicker basket, who had tended him, and raised him, and sent him through high school, mothered and fathered him.

"Okay, I'll try it," Bart had said.

Doc was pleased. "You'll like the Hunters. Dick's the best poker player in the world, or was when I went through the University of Hawaii with him. He may be hard to crack, but once you do, you'll never find a better friend, or father."

It was the last word that had shaken Bart. "Do you mean they are thinking about *adopting* me? No, sir! I'm never going to have any father but you, and no name but Holiday, ever."

"We'll see." Doc's face had held that quizzical smile that Bart had seen so often.

"That's Mauna Kea, an extinct volcano. The Kukaiau ranch, where you're going to live, is on its slopes." Homer's voice recalled Bart to the present. Homer was half Hawaiian and half American, a Forest Reserve ranger, whose Reserve responsibility was right up next to the Kukaiau. He was twenty-one to Bart's seventeen.

"Doc told me," said Bart. He tried to get up, but the seat belt he'd forgotten to unfasten, tossed him back into his chair. Bart grinned and unfastened the belt. "Okay, Holiday," he said under his breath. "Now, let's go." He stood up.

"Take it easy," Homer put a plump brown hand on Bart's arm. "The Hunters won't eat you."

"You sure?" Bart managed to say, as the door of the plane opened and passengers began to file out.

"They're wonderful," Homer said firmly, and led the way.

Bart, stooping a little because he was so tall, followed. He had a small bag in one hand and a caged myna bird in the other. As they moved along, Bart held the bird up and whistled softly into the cage. "Hi, Pete," he said.

"Pete," whom Bart had found injured beneath a magnolia tree, whistled back, as Bart had already taught him to do.

Bart grinned and they reached the exit.

Homer paused there a second, and his eyes met Bart's. "This meeting is tough on you, isn't it?" he said with understanding.

"It's a lot tougher for the Hunters, I suppose. After all, it hasn't been so long since they lost Des."

He looked eagerly east to Mauna Kea. "It's covered with snow at the peak."

"Sure, it's thirteen thousand eight hundred and twenty-five feet high," Homer said. "Just one hundred and forty-five feet higher than Mauna Loa to the south, which is still active. She erupts about every four years." His smile reached Bart. "This is 1950, and she's about due."

They moved down the ramp and toward the gate that would let them out.

Homer, shorter than Bart, had to walk fast to keep up.

"That's the Hunters over there," he said.

Bart looked up, and for a moment he wanted to get right back in the plane and take off. He was scared, just plain scared.

Homer said, "They live on the Kukaiau. Mrs. Hunter knows about all the people who work on the ranch, and there's about a hundred and fifty of them, counting the wives and children."

Bart was hardly listening. He was looking anxiously at Dick Hunter. He saw a medium-sized man with a smooth face and calm blue eyes. His face, browned by the sun, was without a wrinkle, and his mouth wore a pleasant, even smile.

Homer whispered before they reached the Hunters, "Dick's still dazed inside. Can hardly believe that Des is gone."

"Sure, why wouldn't he be?" Bart said and moved forward.

"Of course," Homer agreed. "And he hasn't done anything about the palomino Des was riding either. The horse is just wandering around the ranch or up into the High Country."

"Ruined?"

"His foot, yes. And more than that, his spirit's broken. He's a big golden palomino, descended from a pirate horse who kicked his way free of a ship and fled to the slopes of Mauna Kea. Now, kicked out, and useless, he's on his way out. He won't last long."

"He'll be killed?"

Homer nodded. "That's right, either by lack of water in the High Country, or by a fall, or wild dogs pulling him down."

Bart's eyes, for a swift instant, swept the snow-covered peak of Mauna Kea. "Where's the horse now?" he asked quickly.

"Around the ranch or up in the hills," Homer replied. "Unless he's already gone."

They were through the gate now and walking toward where Mr. and Mrs. Hunter stood waiting. Bart noticed a cheerful-looking young man standing slightly behind them.

"Who's that with them?" he asked Homer.

"Oh, that's Danny Miranda, one of the cowboys. His father, Manuel, is the saddle maker on the Kukaiau and also one of the best ropemakers around."

Then they were in the midst of greetings and introductions. As Bart shook hands with Mrs. Hunter, he was uncomfortably aware of the way her brown eyes searched his face as if she was looking for something special. He wondered nervously what it was.

"How was the trip, Bart?" Mr. Hunter's grip was rope-hard.

"Fine, Mr. Hunter."

"Let's make it 'Dick,' shall we?"

"And I want you to call me 'Helen.'" Helen Hunter was smiling warmly now.

"All right," Bart said, and then wondered if he had sounded ungracious. He wished his stomach would stop tying itself in knots.

"What have you got here?" Dick stooped to look in the cage.

"Pete, my pet myna bird. I had quite a time getting the authorities in Honolulu to let me keep him. It seems there's a law."

"Yes, there's a law," Dick said. "Are you going to train him to talk?"

Bart nodded.

"Well, Larry wrote that we'd have to keep all the animals locked up or they'd be following you all over."

Bart grinned. But a wave of homesickness for Doc in his steel-rimmed spectacles swept over him. "We'll get the bags and get moving," Dick said. "We've got quite a ways to go."

"About ninety miles," Bart said, before he thought.

Dick's face turned to him, pleased, and yet thinking. "Yes, that's right. I see Larry's told you a lot."

"Yes, he has."

There was an awkward pause.

Helen put her hand on Dick's arm and they all moved out to the car, a new Ford station wagon.

Danny Miranda brought the bags.

"Hey, what've you got in this one?" Dick demanded as he stowed it in the back.

"Books, mostly," Bart confessed.

Again Dick seemed pleased. He helped Danny put them in, then opened the front door of the car. Danny and Homer got into the back seat. Bart helped Helen Hunter into the front seat and moved to get in beside her.

But Dick Hunter said, "Oh no you don't," and motioned Bart to come around and get under the wheel. "What do you think I got you up here for?"

For a full minute Bart couldn't move.

Dick Hunter said, "Larry says you're the best driver in all Nebraska."

Bart got under the wheel and gripped it tight. It was a sweet car.

"Doc stretches things sometimes," he said, and stepped softly on the throttle.

They drove north through Honokohau, Puuanahulu, and the Parker ranch.

"Larry used to practice here," Dick said. "He should have stayed. I'd still like to have him back on the island."

"Yes, it would be great," Bart agreed.

He guided the car along the narrow winding road, through wild gooseberry bush and low native trees. They hit open country blackened by lava flows between which grass grew in small plots, and Bart pushed the throttle lower.

"Those are called *kipukas*," Dick explained.

Bart nodded and stepped the car speed up to fifty. They passed close to a little bay much like the one at Kailua.

"Kawaihae," Dick said. "That's where we load cattle for Honolulu."

Bart's hand gripped the wheel tighter, as he caught sight of two cowboys drifting cattle across the ranch. He was such a poor rider, and these men rode like they were part of the saddle. He got a panicky feeling at the pit of his stomach.

"This fall," Dick said, "you'll be in it with us."

Bart gulped. He was no good as a roper. He'd spent his time around the hospital. "Hope so," he managed.

They drove east until they hit the coast and on through miles of sugar cane. As they passed the sugar mill at Paauilo, Dick nodded toward the huge steel structure with the towering crane.

"Friend of mine, Robertson, runs that," he said. Then added, as they sped along, "Robbie's the best, his wife too, and their son, Ian."

At length they turned sharp west and began to climb to a thousand feet, then two, then three, until they reached a big wooden gate Doc had described.

"Now we're entering the Kukaiau," Bart said, almost to himself.

It seemed to him that, as they drove through the gate and on, they entered fairyland. Giant ohia trees were on both sides of the winding, climbing road. They drove through dense woods from which deep-bodied Herefords raised their eyes to stare at the passing car.

Bart knew that they never fed grain, that they sold the beef right off the grass, even before Dick said so.

"I know," Bart said. "The grass is too good. But there's a blight that's slowly taking the range."

"And how did you know that?"

"I've got a book on it," Bart said.

"And some ideas on how to curb it, too, I'll bet," Dick said.

Bart took refuge in paying strict attention to his driving. He didn't want to start sounding like a know-it-all.

They moved on and up around a curve in the road, and there on a flat area, with the sea visible through the trees, lay the long, low ranch house.

Bart's eyes moved around. The barns lay over there and the water tank close by. The corrals lay up the mountainside, or *mauka*, as the natives termed it.

The car rolled to the door and stopped.

Dick got out and helped Helen.

Homer got out too and stood a moment, then said, "I'll take my horse and ride up to camp. There's a flock of nesting nene geese I'm watching."

"Stay tonight," Helen urged.

"Yes, why don't you?" Dick added. "You can go tomorrow. In a few days I'm sending Bart up there to the shack with Danny. That'll be his first chore, to ride herd on some water tanks."

"That's about my speed," Bart said with a grin, and moved to help Danny get the bags.

Wolf, the big German shepherd, came forward to inspect Bart, intently, then sniff at his leg a moment, and finally thrust his nose into Bart's palm.

Dick just stood there and stared before he turned to Helen. "Did you ever see anything like that?" he demanded.

"Never in all the years he's been a dog," Helen declared. "It usually takes from one to three months for him even to notice a stranger."

Bart reddened.

"It figures," Dick said, "from what Doc said. Let's go inside. You, too, Homer."

Bart picked up his bag and walked toward the rambling one-story gray house set in a green lawn amid towering ohia trees.

A cow bawled in the distance. The pad of running horses' feet on the grass came to him. It was all that Doc had said, only Doc hadn't said enough. Bart felt for the first time that he really might want to make good here.

"Boy," he said. "This is wonderful."

But it was so big and there was so much to learn. He tightened his hand on his bag and moved after Helen.

Chapter 2

THE HIDDEN PICTURE

"There'll be a big entry hall with a huge steer's head over the door," Doc had told him.

"And he was so right!" Bart looked up at the biggest steer head he'd ever seen. The horns had a spread of smooth dark-brown bone of well over six feet, above bulging brown eyes and a dun-colored hide.

Bart turned to Helen. "It's a wild steer head?"

"Yes, from the wild herd in the High Country. Up on the slopes of Mauna Kea," Helen said. "There are still some there, though most of them have been killed by wild-dog packs or died of thirst."

"And there are wild horses——" Bart stopped in confusion. For the palomino that had killed Des had been from wild stock.

"Yes, there are wild horses too," Helen said evenly, and led the way down the hall to a room on the left, then through a door.

Bart walked in and knew even before Helen said so

that this had been Des's room. There was a picture of him on the wall, in chaps and with a rope on his arm.

"That picture was taken just a year ago," Helen said quietly.

Bart walked over to look more closely at it. "He looks like a real cowboy," he finally said.

"Yes, he was." Helen smiled.

Bart turned then and spotted the letter from Doc. Even across the room and after an air trip of five thousand miles, Bart caught the faint familiar disinfectant smell. He saw Doc's scrawl across the envelope. He could picture Doc coming in from the operating room with his sleeves rolled up, his hair tousled, and maybe a pup under his arm.

"I'll leave you to unpack," Helen said gently. "The bathroom is there, and the shower, and here's a wardrobe and chiffonier. If there's anything, not enough clothes hooks, or if you want to hang pictures——"

Bart turned to her. Before he thought he put an arm around her shoulders.

"Everything's fine," he said. "Just fine."

"Supper's at seven," she said, and moved out of the door. "Anastasia won't be home until tomorrow. She's visiting in Hilo." She had gone.

Homer came in a few minutes later.

"Mrs. Hunter is pretty special, isn't she?" Bart said thoughtfully.

"Yes," Homer agreed. "She has a lot of courage."

"A lot of women wouldn't have put me in here, in

Des's room," Bart said. He scooped up Doc's letter. "Now, if you'll excuse me, Homer." He sank to a chair and ripped the letter open.

It was so typically a Larry Holiday letter, breezy, but with a lot of things underneath: "Welcome to Kukaiau, you lucky fellow," it started out. "How did you like driving Dick's new Ford?"

Bart swallowed and grinned. The guy was uncanny. Then he was more so. "And how are the butterflies in your stomach?"

Bart had to laugh at that. Then there was some news of the place, things that had been pending when Doc had driven him to the airport: "Bob Matthew's pointer is going to live, but it will be a tough pull. And that little wire-haired terrier with the yippy voice is going home today, thank goodness." There was more of the same about dogs that Bart had tended right up to the last minute.

Bart read on in silence, then reread the last line twice: "Don't think you won't feel green as grass against those trained cowboys. I suppose it'll look as though you've got more to learn than you can handle. But take it easy and keep plugging."

Bart closed the letter and walked over to the window.

Four men rode toward the ranch, herding a bunch of a hundred odd white-faced steers ahead of them.

Homer came over to watch too.

"That's Frank Correia, the foreman since his father died," he explained. "He's wonderful with stock. And there's John Holi Mae, the older man sitting so straight in his saddle. He's the best horse trainer in this area. He's got powerful hands that seem to work some sort of magic with a wild horse."

Bart looked at the men.

"Boy," he said. "Look at the way they handle those cattle, with no yelling. I thought punchers had to yell to get cattle any place."

"They're the best," Homer said.

Bart swung to Des's picture.

"Was he a good roper?" he asked.

"One of the best," Homer said.

Bart turned to Homer, and his stomach felt as though he'd swallowed a saddle blanket. "Think I'll ever learn to ride like those men?"

"Why not?" Homer grinned. "You've got what it takes—a leg for each side of the saddle."

"Watch it," Bart warned, and reached out to lift Homer clear off the floor. "Watch it, or Hawaii and America mainland will have a little private war."

Homer struggled free and Bart started to unpack. He put some things in a little top drawer with paper in the bottom of it. It was an old Honolulu paper that hadn't been put in clean. The maid must have missed taking the old one out.

He started to lift it up, but just then a bell rang.

"Supper," Homer said. "We've got to dash."

The boys dived for the bathroom, then out of the room and down a hall. On the right as they passed lay

the living room with its big lava-rock fireplace, then on
the left and through another door the dining room.

It was a square room with a square mahogany table
and comfortable chairs.

Dick came in and Helen and the two boys.

"You sit there, Homer," Helen said and pointed to a
chair. "*Mauka*, or mountainside," she said to Bart with
a laugh. "That's native for everything up. You see all the
land slopes from Mauna Kea to the sea. Everything is
not up or down, but *mauka* or *makai*."

Bart held her chair, then found his seat, *makai*.

They ate quietly and most of the talk was about Doc.

"A great boy, Doc," Dick said. "A great veterinarian
and an expert with cattle. Guess he never told you this,
but he gave up a good practice here on the island to go
to the States when there was an outbreak of hoof-and-
mouth disease in Texas. He felt it was his duty to go, and
he never got back."

Bart took a drink of water. This was something Doc
had never told him.

When dessert, served by Chris, the little Hawaiian
maid, was over, Helen said, "You'll want to finish un-
packing."

Homer and Helen went to talk before a roaring fire of
ohia logs in the grate, but Dick volunteered to keep Bart
company while he unpacked. He sat on the edge of the
bed and talked while Bart took out his levis and sweat
shirts and hung them in the closets.

"We'll have to get you a Hawaiian hat," he said. "One
for *leis*, like the punchers wear. We've got Chinese,

Hawaiian, and Portuguese punchers from several generations."

"I saw four of them tonight."

"They were bringing the cattle from Tim Field," Dick said. "We've got thirty-four thousand acres here, divided into paddocks of hundreds of acres each. We'll have to get out and see them. What's this?" He picked up a book and read, "*Grasses of the World*. Is this the book you mentioned?"

"That's the one."

Dick thumbed through it, his face intent.

"Maybe you can work it out for us," he said and turned to Bart. "We've got a problem here, as you know. Palmetto is taking the island. Slowly, of course, but surely, and we need to find some way to combat it."

"Some system of replanting a grass that will beat it out?" Bart asked.

"Yes, that's it." Dick nodded. He went down the list of books Bart had put on a table beside his bed: Two books on horse training, a book of the latest fiction; then he picked up a bright red book with gold lettering on it, *The Veterinarian's Handbook*, by Lawrence P. Holiday. A chuckle came from Dick's throat. "P. for Percival," he said. "Imagine not many know that."

"Not many." Bart grinned. He was beginning to enjoy Dick's company.

Dick put the book down abruptly and moved toward the door. Bart realized that he must have done this many times with Des in the past.

"You're in luck, Bart," he said as he paused in the

doorway. "Tomorrow the boys are picking out the new three-year-olds to break for their strings. We can get yours too."

Bart turned to meet Dick's eyes.

"That's wonderful, Dick," he said. He wondered if he sounded as apprehensive as he felt.

Then Dick was gone, and Bart turned to put his clothes in the drawers. He put shirts in one, ties in another, and his small stuff in the top drawer. It was while he was putting things in this one that his hand ruffled the paper he'd found there before supper.

Beneath it he caught sight of a picture. Just the left hind leg of a horse with a bit of pastern, slim and smooth, showing. He pulled the whole picture out. For a moment he stood there and stared at the picture in his hands. It was an enlargement of a snapshot and must have been twelve inches by fourteen.

Homer came in just then and walked over to him. "That's a picture of the Pirate, and that's Des's handwriting beneath it."

Bart's eyes widened as they ran over the clean beauty of the horse. They studied intently the straight back, the fine legs, and slightly dished face of the true Arab horse.

"It figures," he said.

"What?" Homer asked.

"This horse's head, his small ears, and his short-coupled back are so typical. Bet he came from some Arab's band, that stallion that kicked his way free of that pirate ship."

"I don't know," Homer said.

Bart continued to study the picture, then read what Des had written, *The Pirate, Aged Three*. Suddenly he turned to face Homer.

"You know, Des is gone," he said. "And there's no one to look out for this horse. What's going to become of him? Who's going to look out for him?"

"Nobody," Homer said promptly.

"Do you ever see him?" Bart asked.

"I run across him once in a while, mostly up along the volcanic ridge near the Lehu corral." Homer turned to undress. "He's lonely. You know, he's as gentle as a kitten, Bart. He can't figure out what goes on—with all the ranch life and him not in it." Homer dropped a shoe.

Bart put down the picture and started to take off his own shirt. He peeled it over his shock of hair, then stared out of the window. In the light he could see the peak of Mauna Kea glistening under its perpetual snow.

Somewhere up there Pirate stood now. That saddle blanket came back to Bart's stomach again.

"So he's lonely," he said to Homer.

Homer hopped into bed and pulled up the covers.

"Lonely and dazed," he repeated.

Bart snapped out the light and got into the twin bed beside Homer's.

"You know, Bart," Homer said and raised to an elbow. "You don't know it yet. But really you've got yourself two jobs here on the ranch."

Bart stared up at the ceiling. "You mean making

good as a cowboy and pulling the Pirate back into things? Those would have been Des's jobs," he added to himself.

"You figure it out," Homer said and turned on his side.

"But how do I know I can fix his foot? How do I know Dick Hunter'll want me to?"

Homer didn't answer. His slow, regular breathing told Bart that he was already asleep. He suddenly realized that he faced things alone.

Chapter 3

CORRAL DECISION

The low bellow of a Kukaiau bull wakened Bart.

He sprang out of bed to walk toward the window, pausing a moment to put a finger into Pete's cage and say, softly, "Hello, hello, hello, that's your lesson for today, boy."

Once at the window, he stared out into the early morning light.

"Hey," he said to Homer. "Do you see what I see?"

Homer came over to stand beside him. "Oh, that maverick," he said and yawned, then crawled back into bed for another forty winks.

"Yes, that maverick." Bart continued to stare at the little gray horse that stood slack-hipped against the hill, not feeding, not doing anything. He was gray, that much was sure, and a horse, but that was about all. He had a ragged mane and a head much too big for his body.

"Skip it," Homer said, a trifle irritated at not being able to go back to sleep. "He's the joke of the ranch. Just a raw green colt with a loose hide, a glass eye, and a skinny body that appeared out of nowhere. Mr. Hunter's selling him down to the sugar plantation this week, I believe."

Bart turned to dress, then changed the water in Pete's cage and threw him some seeds, but the gray stuck in his mind.

"Well, here we go," Homer said, and slid from bed to race into his khaki uniform.

"I smell breakfast," Homer said. "Come on."

They moved out of the door, with Bart saying as he passed Pete, "Keep practicing, 'Hello, hello, hello.' I'll be back."

Dick and Helen were waiting in the dining room. They stood beside the window looking at the sunlight that struggled for a chance against the slow-moving fog in the ohia trees.

Dick turned as the two boys came into the room. He wore khaki and a flannel shirt. It was evident that he'd been up for hours. It was April, and calving time, and the days were all too short for all that had to be done.

"Good morning, boys," he said, and motioned them to the table.

Bart leaped to pull the chair out for Helen, then sat down at her right.

While they ate, Dick outlined the day.

"We'll go up to the corral right away," he said. "Then we'll take the four-wheel-drive Ford and go into the High Country. I'll show you the place and drop you off at the Sky Camp."

"Dick, so soon?" Helen protested. "Bart's only just come."

"I've been on a plane for days," Bart said quickly. "Let's go."

Dick nodded his satisfaction. "You can ride with us to Sky Camp, Homer," Dick went on. "Danny can trail your horse along with the two colts he'll take up for you two boys to break."

Bart polished off his bacon and eggs. Suddenly he could hardly wait to get up there and start his work on the ranch.

"Sounds great," he said.

"Well, it won't be very exciting work," Dick warned him. "We have droughts here and we've built tanks to catch and store rain water. It's precious. So we have installed a system of floats in the tanks to let just the right amount of water into the troughs as the cattle use it. You'll be checking the tanks."

"Yippee!" Homer exclaimed, and grinned at Bart. "Rid'n' the old water troughs."

"I'll see you outside," Bart said with a fake scowl.

"Boys, boys," Helen said, and they all laughed.

They finished breakfast in silence after that.

In half an hour Dick led Bart out across the road to the harness shop.

A little dark-skinned man with lively eyes and the most supple hands Bart had ever seen turned on his stool as they entered. Before him lay a tanned cowhide which he was cutting in circular strips. Across a rack behind him stood a series of bare saddletrees waiting for the leather.

"We make our own saddletrees of sumac wood," Dick said to Bart. "I can brag because Manuel here makes them. Bart, this is Manuel Miranda, Danny's father, and our saddle and ropemaker. Manuel, this is Bart Holiday, who's come to help us on the ranch."

"I'm glad to know you, Manuel," Bart said and shook hands, then turned to finger the soft leather strips Manuel had cut from the cowhide. Again, as he touched it, came that sense of apprehension. For this would be a lariat, and what did he know about throwing a rope?

"I don't know much about tanning," he said. "But it certainly feels soft to me." He bent to watch Manuel continue to cut the leather in a circular motion.

"You'll know more," Dick promised. "But now we've got to get up to the corral and get you a horse to ride."

They moved to go, but suddenly Manuel reached into a cupboard and brought out a wonderful newly-braided rope forty feet long with a braided honda.

"For you," he said, and pressed it into Bart's astonished hands.

"Hey!" Bart protested.

"It's all right," Dick assured Bart. "It's for you."

"But—but I only just came."

"Manuel's known you were coming for some time. This is his way of saying, 'Welcome to Kukaiau.'"

Bart swallowed hard as he clutched the rope. He had the feeling that it was a solid band that bound him closer to the ranch.

"Here's your saddle," Dick said.

Bart hefted the heavy stock saddle with the plain unstamped leather, then put it down. What would happen the first time he used it?

"We'll pick it up later," Dick said, and moved to go.

Bart pressed the old ropemaker's hand again.

"Thanks, Manuel," he said.

"You come see me," Manuel said. "Often." He pointed to the door. "She is always open—for you."

Dick got outside and scratched his head.

"I don't know," he said. "I'll have to watch you. You'll have my job here in no time. First Wolf makes up fast, and now Manuel. Both hard to crack and they're wide open for you."

Bart flushed clear down into his blue wool shirt. There was nothing he could say. He could only walk after Dick up through the trees and along a path to the corrals. There were big corrals to hold the cattle, and smaller corrals for branding, and chutes for cutting, all of ohia wood.

Dick pointed to a small round corral that led from one of the main ones.

"This is where we do the branding," he said. "That'll be in June. By then you should be handling a rope and a horse pretty well."

Bart felt small and helpless.

Then suddenly down through the trees, like a bunch of schoolboys, came the three-year-old colts that were ready to be broken to the saddle. There were twenty of them, mostly geldings.

"They run to bays and sorrels," Dick explained. "Out

of our stallion, Sturdy Defense." He pointed to a light
sorrel that led the rest. The colt had a blazed face and
clean legs. "He's like his daddy," Dick said. "That's the
colt for you."

Bart nodded, but he kept watching the little gray ghost
maverick who came out of the woods and ran to join
the horses, then trailed them into the corral.

Bart recognized Frank Correia, the foreman, smiling
Danny, and John Holi Mae. And Dick pointed out Kim
Lee, a Chinese, Herman Naipo, a Hawaiian, and several
others.

"Larry could never get over us having Chinese cow-
punchers," Dick said with a laugh. "But they're as good
as they come, and natural cow handlers."

Suddenly the gate banged shut and Dick led Bart
down to the corral and inside.

"Boys," he said, "this is Bart Holiday who's come to
help us here on the ranch."

Bart shook hands all around and found himself
hemmed in by the punchers. He felt smothered and alien.

"How do you do," he said stiffly.

"He lives with Doc Holiday, whom you all remember,"
Dick said.

They all grinned and nodded vigorously.

Dick smiled. "You see, Bart, Larry rates around here."

Bart couldn't take his eyes off the little gray horse
in the corral. The sorrel had bitten him deep along his
withers and taken a piece of hide off. The little colt was
being kicked along from one colt to another.

Then Dick turned to Bart. "You're the newcomer here.
You get first pick."

Bart, startled, shook his head. "Hey, no! Let Danny
here or John Holi Mae pick first, but not me."

The atmosphere was suddenly warm and friendly.

"Okay," Dick said quietly. "We'll take the usual turns
then."

Bart hoped that someone else would draw the sorrel.
But he could see that as each stepped up they purposely left him for Bart.

At length Danny had a bay, John Holi Mae another
sorrel, Kim a black, and so on down the line.

"Now, Bart," Dick said.

There wasn't much left but the two colts: the big
sorrel with the white-stocking feet, and the little gray
horse with the big head and glass eye.

Bart stepped forward. He could almost hear Doc say,
"Don't be a chump, Bart. Take the sorrel."

Bart gulped. He stepped up and pointed to the gray.

John Holi Mae's guttural voice exclaimed under his
breath. Then a silence drifted over the corral.

It made Dick look foolish, as though he'd taken a boy
who wasn't too bright.

Bart forced a grin and pulled the little gray to him.

"We'll start from the ground up," he said. "Glass eye
and all."

Dick's face said a thousand things. But he came
through.

"It figures," he said softly and chuckled. "Larry said

you had a way of going for the underdog." He turned to the cowboys. "All right, boys. I'll take the sorrel for myself."

Bart knew then how much he liked Dick Hunter. He grinned ruefully. "I ought to have my head examined."

"Maybe." Dick smiled back. "But we'll have to get Larry to do that."

It was settled then.

Bart slipped his new rope over the little gray's head and led him from the corral and down to the saddling shed. And there at one end of the long rail just back of the horses was a green locker with B. Holiday painted on it in white letters.

Bart stared at it, and there was that blanket in his stomach again.

"You'll learn," Dick said softly.

Bart didn't know. He felt like a chump already. But he slipped his hand along the rough hide of the colt and gave it a pat. "I hope I learn. But about choosing this colt, I had to do it. I've got him and we'll learn this thing together."

"The hard way," Dick said.

"The hard way!" Bart agreed.

Dick turned to the door. "All right. Now we'll take the car and pick up Homer and take off for High Country."

Chapter 4

THE PIRATE

In an hour they'd loaded the four-wheel-drive Ford truck with food and picked up Homer.

Bart thanked Helen, who stood in the doorway, for her offer to look after Pete.

"Danny's trailing your colt and his own, along with Homer's horse, up to Sky Camp," Dick said. "There's bedding there and everything you'll need to cook with."

Bart smiled. "I hope Danny's a good cook."

"Don't kid me," Dick said. "Larry's written about your waffles and hot cakes." He opened the car door for Bart to get behind the wheel.

"Oh no, not this time. Not right up there," Bart objected.

"All right then, *this* time." Dick got behind the wheel.

They drove north through a gate, past the corrals, and then, it seemed to Bart, straight up. He glanced ahead at the dim trail that wound through ohia trees and over volcanic humps. He'd never seen such wonderful country in his life.

No wonder Doc had been so crazy about it. Bart recalled the enthusiasm in his voice as he described the wild-hog wallows, the volcanic formations, the white-faced cattle among the trees.

Bart sat and watched the trees go by as the truck climbed the wild terrain.

"You know, Dick," he said, between bumps of the truck, "Doc told me about this, but he didn't half cover it."

Dick skillfully guided the car around a cattle wallow. "No?"

"It seems like there are calves everywhere."

"We've had a good crop this spring—about eighty-five per cent, I think. We won't know until branding time."

"And all polled Herefords, the aristocrats of the cow world," Bart said.

Dick seemed pleased at this tribute to the Kukaiau herd.

They moved on up the trail that all but petered out to nothing, through ohia trees that suddenly changed to koa trees with wide-spreading branches much like the oak.

"Koa country?" Bart queried.

"Right." Dick said. "Above thiry-five hundred and up to seventy-five hundred."

"And above that?" Bart braced himself against the jolt of the careening truck.

"My country," Homer put in. "That's the Mauna Kea Forest Preserve."

Dick grinned.

"He's really too modest, Bart," he said. "Homer covers that area and the sea for poachers. He's got a little ranch too, down by the City of Refuge, below Kealakekua Bay."

"City of Refuge?"

"Yes," Homer said. "A point of land established and put aside by past Hawaiian kings. Anyone who could make it to this little point of land jutting into the sea, in time of war, had sanctuary. Sometime, when I'm going down there, I'll take you."

"Maybe you can take Bart with you in your outrigger when you're looking for poachers or thieves raiding the burial caves for artifacts?" Dick suggested.

"Artifacts?" Bart asked.

"Yes, old implements of cooking and warfare of the Hawaiian tribes," Homer explained. "My people buried them in these lava caves or tubes with the bodies."

"Lava tubes are formed by lava cooling from the outside, and the inside lava flowing on, thus leaving a tube or cave," Dick said with a laugh. "Now you know it all, Bart."

"Not quite," Homer said, and looked south to Mauna Loa lying in a bank of fleecy white clouds. "He hasn't seen an eruption. And," he added, "let's hope it will be a long time before he does."

They drove on and at length passed through a gate.

"We're leaving the Corn Field paddock, two thousand and seventy acres," Dick explained. "And entering

Papa, nine hundred acres. Above Papa is Apoo Puaa, then Iolemaehae, where Sky Camp is located."

"And may I have the next dance?" jibed Homer. "Did you ever hear such names, Bart?"

"You'll get on to them," Dick said. "Once you learn that every letter is sounded."

"It's no worse than Wrdzlyski, Nebraska." Bart laughed.

"Where's that?" Homer queried.

"How should I know? All I did was express a terrier pup to a man there once," Bart replied.

They pulled up beside a cement trough and Dick got out.

Bart followed.

They walked across the soft grass to the tank that stood with water just to the right level within. Several cows moved from it to look back at the two men. Two calves frisked behind their mothers, then ran bawling up the hillside.

Dick walked over to the trough and pressed down on a small lever to the end of which was connected a big float.

"This is the thing you watch, Bart," he said. "See that this doesn't stick and waste valuable water. Of course, Danny will be with you part of the time. But you might as well learn." Dick turned to point up the hill to a big wooden tank with a cement drainage apron feeding into it. "There's the storage tank. Remember, if that goes dry, the cattle will die of thirst."

Bart suddenly remembered the Pirate. Was he dying of thirst?

They got back into the truck. But someway the trees didn't look so green now, or the sun so bright, for Bart. He could see what Homer had meant about the Pirate now, when he said, "It's pretty grim for him."

They drove on to Sky Camp, by way of four other tanks, then along a hogback to the cabin.

Once a bunch of wild pigs crossed their path. They grunted and scurried from a hillside, which had been furrowed and torn by their snouts.

Another time Bart knew he'd have been thrilled at sight of them as they dashed for the bush. Now he just sat dumbly in the car and looked straight ahead. He couldn't help thinking what could happen to Pirate if the weather got dry.

At last they sighted the roof of a little brown-boarded two-roomed cabin with a sheet-metal roof. Around it was a fenced paddock and a small stable. Off to the right and down the hill lay the huge cement apron that fed into a gigantic new steel water tank.

Upgrade lay a fence.

"That's the division line between the Kukaiau and the Forest Reserve," Homer said.

It was four wires high with posts a rod apart, and no horse, or any other animal, could knock it down or go through it.

"No matter how thirsty he was," Bart told himself.

Dick drove up and pulled on the brakes.

They all got out and began to unload the truck. In fifteen minutes Dick was ready to take the straight seven-mile road back to the ranch.

"We came up by the tanks," he said. "I can make it home in half an hour." He pointed to the telephone. "Danny'll be up soon. Should be here by now. There's the telephone in case you want to call the ranch." He paused a moment, then said, "Well, so long, Bart," and got into the truck.

Bart watched Dick drive down through the koa trees, and his arm still tingled with the pressure of Dick's hand on it. But then he heard a noise behind him and turned around. For a full ten seconds, there in the dappled sunlight, he stared at the horse before him.

The palomino was leaning over the fence, his grace-ful neck pressed up against the wires until they sagged under his weight. Bart guessed it at around twelve hundred pounds. He had the dish face of the Arab, the fine limbs, and the wide-spaced eyes. His body was pure gold, and his flaxen mane and tail stirred slightly in the soft mountain breeze.

He pawed slightly and nickered, and he couldn't have said any plainer, "Hi, how are you?" if he'd been able to talk.

Bart moved to the fence as though drawn by a magnet. He put a hand along the palomino's muscled neck and said, over and over, "Pirate! Pirate! Pirate!"

Homer came out of the cabin.

"I guess you can see what I meant now, when I said you had two jobs, can't you?"

Bart's hand tightened, then he moved along the fence to open the gate and let Pirate into the paddock beside the cabin. He picked up Pirate's right front foot and looked at the hoof.

"Yes, I can see," he said. Suddenly he knew that he really did have two things he *wanted* to accomplish. One, to get to know the ranch and become a cowboy who could drag his own weight, and the other, to get this horse back on four good feet and at work on the ranch.

He examined the shriveled frog and the side of the hoof torn away.

"That'll never grow back," Homer said.

"No, maybe not," Bart agreed. He'd seen something of horses' hoofs as he'd worked around Bateman's blacksmith shop just behind Doc's hospital. Doc had had a case or two that he'd helped care for.

He dropped Pirate's foot to the ground and turned around to watch Danny trail the colts and Homer's horse into the yard.

"I'll pare the hoof down, soak it in water and oil, and try to stimulate growth," he said. "I'll write Doc too. He'll know what to do."

Homer went to get his horse and mounted.

"I hope so," he said as he rode back to Bart. "If he doesn't, Pirate's a goner."

Chapter 5

STUBBORN HOPE

Bart turned to go to the shack, but the sound of a motor stopped him, and there was Dick Hunter coming back up the road in the four-wheel drive.

He braked the car to a halt and for a moment nothing was said. Then he got out of the car and came over to Bart.

"I know you must have wondered why I haven't done more for Pirate," he said. "But it's no good, Bart." He looked off into the trees. "It isn't that I lost interest in Pirate because—because of Des," he went on. Suddenly he walked over to pick up Pirate's injured foot and with his pocketknife dug out the pumice and stones that had collected along the injured frog. "I've had a veterinarian look at it. Necombe, a man who is the best in the game from Honolulu. I even had one from New Zealand who was here."

Dick dug around the hoof, with the horse breaking into a nervous sweat as he worked.

"See here," he said.

But Pirate reared and pulled away.

Dick brought him back and lifted the hoof once more.

"Easy boy, easy," he said, and motioned Bart to come close.

Bart bent down and tried to see the hoof, but all he could think about was Pirate under a saddle.

"The frog's almost gone," Dick said and pointed to it with his knife blade.

Bart managed to focus on it. He knew what a hoof should look like, but he wouldn't admit that this was so bad.

"I thought with massage and hot oil and care——"

"But Necombe of Honolulu says the nerve's been injured," Dick protested.

"Even nerves come back," Bart said. He couldn't believe that Pirate was through. He wouldn't.

"Yes, in a way."

"But maybe with shoes he'll come around," Bart went on. "I've fooled around with the forge at Bateman's blacksmith shop. I've seen some of Bateman's horses come along fine."

"Necombe went into that, too," Dick said. "A shoe built up on that side would be too heavy." He let the foot down to stand beside the horse. "Look, Bart. You can see daylight clear up one side of his foot. It would take a lot of iron there, and then it wouldn't hold. There's nothing to nail to." He stooped to run the blade of his knife along the hoof line and down into the dirt.

Bart was careful to show respect for Dick, who honestly

believed what he was saying. He bent to inspect the hoof, but he wouldn't believe what he saw. He didn't dare.

Dick stood up.

"In some countries a shoe might work," he said. "Where the horse walks on grass. But here with this pumice and among these *kipukas*, with the horse hitting solid rock at high speed, there isn't a chance. So forget it, Bart."

Bart stood erect. He faced Dick.

"And anyway"—Dick's face showed concern—"beyond all this, suppose you did get the right shoe that was the right weight and managed to put it on the horse, there's still the nerve angle." He gently slapped Pirate's neck. The horse ran a few feet, then limped back to them.

Bart did not move. He could only see the ripple of muscle along that neck and the flash of those brown eyes. This horse had to live. He had to.

"I didn't want to tell you this, Bart," Dick said slowly. "But I'll have to let you have it all as Doctor Necombe explained it to me. There'll always be a limp. Get the right shoes of the right weight, and everything else correct, and what have you got?"

"A cow horse!" Bart almost shouted the words. "A wonderful cow horse who'll show the way to all the rest, at branding, at cattle loading at Kawaihae."

But Dick's voice cut in, "No, a limping horse, and what good is a limping horse here?"

"Limps have been cured," Bart said. He put a hand along Pirate's neck and everything became a blur to him. He could only see one thing. "I hate to be so obstinate," he said. "But do you mind if I try?"

"For Des?" Dick asked, with a flash of understanding.

Bart's voice came so softly you could hardly hear it. "Yes, and for Pirate and for you and me, and for all of us who love horses."

Still Dick hesitated.

Then he smiled and put a hand on Bart's arm. "I can see you're going to do it anyway, just the way you chose Ghost. I might as well say yes."

Bart was already embarrassed by his own stubbornness. "I, well, well——"

"Forget it. It's settled." Dick moved to his car and got behind the wheel.

"On my own time then," Bart said. "I won't shirk my work, and anything I do will be after hours."

Dick waved an arm.

"We won't worry about that. And you can have the use of the blacksmith shop and shoes if you need them —the works." He let the car in gear and gunned the motor. Then leaned out to add, "There's oil in the shack, and good luck." His voice, as he said it, might have added, "You'll need it, and more."

He drove away. Bart stood beside Pirate. Danny appeared around the cabin.

"We make a horse of him, you bet," he said, and pulled Pirate's flaxen mane.

The horse snorted and backed away.

"You bet, if he'll let us," Bart said, with more conviction than he felt. He turned toward the cabin. He'd write Doc, and in the meantime, he'd try oil and massage and cleanliness.

Danny and Bart cooked supper and washed the dishes, then Bart got out his mouth organ and began to play.

Suddenly the cabin door burst open and Pirate thrust his muzzle inside.

"So you like music?" Bart said, and played "Sweet Sue," then "The Long, Long Trail," for the stallion. At length he knocked his harmonica against his hand and stood up. "Concert's over for tonight," he said, and stepped out into the dark.

Even in Nebraska he'd always done this before going to bed. It gave him a moment with himself and the stars.

He stared up at the sky dotted by millions of twinkling lights, as the big golden Pirate limped over to nudge him with his soft nose. Bart thrust an arm around his neck and pulled his head around.

"Tomorrow we start on you," he said. "And you'd better be good, see?"

Pirate shook his head and riffled a button on Bart's jacket between his teeth, then followed Bart as far as the cabin door.

Chapter 6

LETTER TO DOC

The next morning after breakfast Bart walked out of the cabin and toward the little gray Ghost and Pirate who grazed close together. He had Manuel's new rope on his arm.

A bright sun shone down and dappled the landscape beneath the trees. To the east, the sea glistened like a huge blue mirror.

Bart walked close to Pirate and slapped him along the neck.

"How about it?" he queried. "Are you going to be good when you have your foot treatment tonight?"

The big horse nickered and all but tossed Bart off balance with a thrust of his muzzle to his chest.

Bart straightened up and let his eyes move around a half circle. There were trees everywhere, and beneath them polled Herefords with calves by their sides. He drew a deep breath and let it out.

"Pretty big, this ranch," Danny said as he came to stand beside Bart.

Bart nodded. For the first time he felt the size of the Kukaiau.

"Yes, sir," he said, "it is," then added to himself, "and I'm a part of it."

"Wait until we round up the cattle in June," Danny said as he reached his black to put a rope around his neck. "Then you'll see how big: six miles each way and six thousand head of cattle all going down the mountain together."

"Did you say wait?" Bart said with a grin. "With all I have to do between now and then?"

Danny's broad smile answered him.

Bart walked to put his rope around Ghost's thin gray neck and led him back to the cabin.

The big golden horse moved along with the two as they came back to camp. He ran ahead, then trailed behind and seemed puzzled that no one threw a rope on him too.

"He can't understand it," Danny said.

Bart drew in his breath, and walked a little faster.

"We'll fix that," he said. "Beginning tonight. But right now, there's this little guy who's got to have some know-how put into his big head."

They reached the camp.

Bart watched Danny and followed his instructions.

"Some ranches put a saddle on a wild horse, then get on and make him buck and break him that way," Danny said, then shook his head. "But the Kukaiau is different. We do it like this." He put a rope on his black

and led him around the yard for a few times. He talked
to him. He leaned his body on the black.

Bart did the same with the gray. But the little colt, green
and scrawny, all but keeled over.

"Hey, I'll have to prop you up against a koa tree,"
Bart exclaimed.

Danny's laugh rang through the trees as they went on
with their training. After two hours Danny slipped his
rope from the black. "Now we'll ride the tanks," he said.

Bart looked down the hill to the big steel thirty-
thousand-gallon tank.

"Oh yeah, I'm not bowlegged enough for that."

Danny joined in his laugh, and they went to saddle the
two horses Danny had brought up for them to use until
his black and Ghost should be ready to ride.

Bart tossed the Navaho blanket that Doc had given
him on the bay he'd use, then his saddle. He cinched it
up, while all the time Pirate kept nosing around.

"He might just as well say, 'Why don't you saddle
me?'" Bart told Danny. It made Bart anxious to get
going.

Danny nodded, and the two boys rode out of the yard.

Pirate wanted to come, but Bart put him in the paddock and shut the gate.

"You stay here, and I'll see you tonight," he promised.

Danny led the way and they eased down the mountainside to check all the tanks and water troughs. Then they
rode through the cows and calves to check the new
calf crop.

"It's part of the job to see that none of them are in trouble," Danny explained.

With that done, Danny swung *mauka* again.

"Now we ride the fence line," he said. "Sometimes the cattle get through and go with the wild cattle."

Bart's eyes moved toward the gently sloping mountain.

"Are there still wild cattle up there?" he asked.

"A few," Danny said. "But the drought has killed most of them. That and the wild dogs."

"And the horses too?" Bart couldn't help asking, though Helen had told him the same thing.

"Yes," Danny said. "There aren't many left. Once in a while a stray band, but not often."

Bart pushed his bay faster along the fence line. He had to get going on Pirate, he could see that. For let the horse give up entirely and it would be only a question of time until he'd stray up there and be killed.

They rode in silence for the four miles of the upper fence line, then started back to camp.

It was five o'clock by the time they reached home. "You go ahead," Danny insisted. "I'll cook supper."

"Not a chance," Bart protested. "That can wait."

He helped Danny cook sweet potatoes, rice, and ham, then sat down to eat. After supper he carefully took a brush and curry comb and walked out to Ghost.

"Okay, little guy," he said. "Here's where we begin to make you look like a horse that somebody cares for."

He worked for an hour, brushing and grooming the

thin gray horse. He put the brush and comb away and examined Ghost's teeth to see that they were sound and didn't need filing down.

Doc's words, "Any horse can be made to respond to treatment if his teeth are right," came back to Bart.

Bart took his hands free of the colt and wiped them on a rag. "I wish mine were half as good, Ghost," he said, "and I'll see you tomorrow."

He turned to Pirate.

"Now, boy," he said. "We'll give you a whirl."

He brought the hot water and the oil he'd found in the cabin. He put his rope on Pirate and led him close to the steps.

"Now this won't hurt you," he said and tried to put the big stallion's foot in the bucket.

But the horse, suspicious of anything that had to do with his sore foot, backed away and snorted in alarm.

Bart tried again, and he ran down the slope and dragged Bart after him.

Bart brought him back.

"It's for you, boy," he begged. "See?" He plunged his own hand into the bucket.

Pirate nosed Bart's hat nervously, then nibbled his arm.

"What's going on here?" he seemed to say.

"Plenty, I hope," Bart said and tried again.

It was not until a half-moon was sitting in the Hawaiian sky that Bart got the foot in the bucket and later applied the hot oil.

"That's all for tonight, Pirate," he said, as he emptied the bucket. "See you tomorrow night, and every night until June fourth, roundup time."

Bart moved toward the cabin and tried not to see Pirate's limp as the big horse joined Ghost along the hillside.

Inside, Danny lay on his bunk reading a magazine. Bart slumped to a chair and pulled some paper out of a drawer to write Doc.

He would be going the rounds with the dogs about now, stroking one, patting another. The little fox terrier with the boil in his throat would be yipping his head off and trying to commit suicide by crawling through the wire separating his kennel from Amory Water's white pit bull.

Bart settled to his writing. He stared out of the window and caught the silhouette of Pirate.

"Dear Doc," he began. "Well, here I am, and what you said about this place wasn't half enough. Dick and Helen, as they've asked me to call them, are the greatest." He paused a moment. "Doc, you've got to help me. You've just got to. Remember the horse that Des was riding when he was killed? Well, he's big and gentle and crippled. He tore his foot in that lava tube. It'll never be right. But I've got to do something, don't you see? Or he'll go to pieces and die. I'm soaking the foot in hot water and oil. Maybe you can tell me what to do. Perhaps some shoes or a cast or something——" Bart went on describing the foot and then his work. He told about Ghost, the little gray waif he'd chosen, and how he'd been afraid he'd made Dick Hunter seem like a chump. At last he signed his name at the bottom of the second sheet and stuffed it in an envelope and addressed it.

Dick would pick it up in the morning, Bart decided and figured that he should get an answer in ten days. At last he stowed his paper away and walked outside.

Pirate raised his head to nicker, then limped over to Bart.

Suddenly Homer came out of the darkness and stood to watch the palomino come down to them.

"Thought I'd drop by to tell you that I'll be away for a few days," he said.

Bart touched Pirate's nose and turned to Homer.

"Trouble?" he asked.

"Poaching down at the City of Refuge area," Homer said. "Some thieves rifling lava tubes for artifacts to bootleg to unscrupulous dealers."

Bart thought of his letter. Mailing it at Kailua might cut off a day or so in hearing from Doc. He told Homer what he'd written.

"Maybe you'd mail it for me?" he asked.

"Glad to," Homer replied.

Bart got the letter and asked Homer to come in. But Homer had to get on. Pocketing the letter, he turned to go. "Anything else I can do?"

"No, thanks," Bart said. Time was so precious for Pirate he was grateful to Homer.

"*Aloha*, good-by, then," Homer said and moved off into the night.

Bart opened the door and walked inside to undress and crawl in beside Danny. He lay staring up at the ceiling, and ten days seemed like a long time to wait for Doc's reply.

Chapter 7

BETTER TO SHOOT HIM

Two weeks later Bart walked out into the yard of Sky Camp. Today they were going to move cattle from one paddock to another and he hoped he wouldn't make too many blunders.

Danny came up beside him as they reached the horses that they were breaking. He put his hand along Ghost's neck that had already filled out and shone with the work of Bart's nightly currying.

"You're sure making a horse out of him," Danny said. "And just in time. We'll test him today."

Bart looked across to Pirate who limped toward him, then down the trail for a sight of Dick who might bring him a letter from Doc.

"Yes," he said, and tried to smile. "And he isn't the only one to be tested."

"Oh, you'll do all right," Danny said. "Just keep behind the cows so they won't think they're herding you. And remember the things we've been practicing for two weeks." He laughed and walked on to slip a rope on his bay.

Bart led Ghost down to the cabin and saddled up.

Pirate came along. He nudged Ghost to one side and bit him playfully, then stood waiting for Bart to toss his saddle on him.

"If I only could," Bart said. "Your time will come, boy. Doc'll tell us what to do." He finished saddling the gray, then put his bridle on and mounted.

Voices through the trees made Bart turn in his saddle. Soon the punchers would ride up into the field and the drive would begin, and he felt as green as range grass.

The boys' colts were green. They wouldn't neck-rein too well. They handled themselves awkwardly and turned sidewise at the touch of the reins along their necks. They moved crablike down the trail, but they didn't buck or rear and were doing all right for two weeks under the saddle.

Frank Correia led the cowboys into the yard. Bart couldn't help but admire the way he sat his horse. He was lean and lithe and brown and he knew cattle.

Bart was beginning to have a great deal of respect for these men who hit the saddle six days a week, rain or shine, handled cattle without raising their voices, and knew every inch of the Kukaiau as well as they knew their own back yards.

"Just make me half as good," he said. "And get me through today."

"We'll move the cattle from Saddle Horse Pen to Apoo Puaa," Frank said as he drew rein before the cabin. "It's the first step toward branding in June."

Branding! Brother! Bart's eyes met Danny's. There was so much yet to learn.

Danny winked as Frank dropped from his saddle.

"I'll telephone Mr. Hunter," he said. "Then we'll go." He reached the cabin steps, then suddenly turned toward Bart.

"How much water in the big tank?" he asked.

It was a simple question, put as one puncher to another about the work.

"About half a tank, sir," Bart replied proudly.

"And number two, down at Apoo Puaa?"

"The same, maybe a little less," Bart said.

"Kukaiau, Kaala, Jack Field?" Frank went through them all.

Bart gave the answers. He could see now that what he'd been doing wasn't just child's play. The lives of thousands of cattle, the life of the ranch itself, depended on keeping the water under control.

"All right, I'll speak to Mr. Hunter," Frank said. "Then we'll drift."

Bart took off the Hawaiian cowboy hat that Dick had given him. It was a little damp around the band where it had touched his forehead. Suppose he hadn't been able to answer Frank's questions!

Danny grinned and winked again.

"It'll come easier after a while," he said.

Bart reddened but breathed easier as the men around him pretended not to notice. He could hear the "Brrr!"

of the telephone, then Frank's voice. In five minutes they were off.

Frank came out and eased into his saddle, lithe as a puma. He swung his horse and, with John Holi Mae, led them down the trail and east.

They rode silently but steadily on, through sleek cows and calves that nudged their mothers' udders.

Once Bart heard the grunt of wild pigs as they grubbed for roots along the hillsides, heard their swift rush of feet and squeals as they fled through the trees.

Two weeks before he'd have been excited. Now he barely turned his head and thought mostly of the drive ahead.

He looked sharply at a water hole as they passed.

Frank noticed it too.

"Down," he said, as one puncher to another, and glanced anxiously at the sky. "Let's not have another drought like the one of 'forty-seven when we had to haul a million gallons of water up the mountain."

Bart nodded, and he suddenly realized that he'd mentally registered this water hole of his own accord. He felt better. There was method in Dick's sending him up there with Danny to act as instructor.

He rode on with Frank as the sun climbed higher, and a soft wind rustled the trees, and the low of cattle followed them.

At the far end of Saddle Horse Pen, Frank turned in his saddle.

"I'll take Bart," he said. "John, you and Danny ride

up to the division fence and move everything east. Keoki
and Kim, you ride south to the border and work east."

They nodded.

"Bart and I'll take the middle," Frank finished.

Bart flushed and his hands froze to his reins. This was
it—the big test.

"It gets you," Frank said with a glance at Bart's face.

"It surely does."

Bart rode with Frank as they started east.

"This field has about two thousand acres in it," Frank
said. "We'll be moving around a thousand head of cattle
before night."

"A thousand head!"

After a few hundred feet, Frank swung to Bart.

"Fan out now," he said, "and keep a sharp lookout for
single cows with several calves lying in the brush. They
do that, you know; take turns watching while the others
graze. Don't crowd the herd or make any false moves
either. They're getting fat and run easily."

"I know," Bart said, glad that Danny had taught him
as much as he had.

He guided Ghost to the right and off toward some
trees. He rode to a cinder cone and around it. He felt
strange for a moment and didn't know what the feeling
meant. Then he realized. He was on his own. A puncher
on his first drive.

For a moment he reined up. He put his hand along
Ghost's neck. If only you were Pirate. "But that's not
fair," he said. "Little horse, let's get going."

He saw a bunch of cattle ahead. There were half a dozen cows with calves and a couple of two-year-old steers. The latter were already fat, but nothing to what they would be in October, when they drove them to Kawaihae for shipment to Honolulu.

Bart rode toward them, easing them forward as Danny had already taught him on their rides to check the water tanks.

"Hi! Ki yyaa yippee!" He opened his mouth to yell, then closed it, glad that he hadn't shouted. The Hawaiian way was quiet, with not a sound; with only the steady pressure of good cowmen on know-how horses at the right place at the strategic time.

Bart rode back of the cows and calves and the two steers and began weaving back and forth, pushing the stock ahead of him.

Off to his left, Frank on his roan did likewise.

Slowly the herd began to move. All along the fence the cattle began, almost without knowing it, to move toward the gate in the middle of the field.

The sun climbed higher, with no clouds in the sky except that perpetual white veil that hovered around Mauna Kea's peak.

Through the trees Bart could see the ocean. Off to the north lay the sharp edge of Maui, with its giant mountain, Haleakala. North of that again lay the leper island, Molokai.

Then the sun reached its zenith. The cattle grew into a herd. Calves lost their mothers and set up a crescendo of sound. Mothers bawled for calves. Calves bawled for cows.

Still the riders pushed forward and took the cattle before them. At length they were through the first gate and across Halipilua Paddock. The sun began its long slide into the sea.

At four, they crossed the twelve-hundred-and-sixty-acre paddock to reach another gate. Slowly, with infinite patience, the riders began pushing the cattle through it. Bart worked his gray with them.

"Just get them through this gate," he told Danny, as they rode stirrup to stirrup. "That's all I ask."

"Don't let Frank hear you say that?" Danny replied and flicked his rope at a lagging calf. "He's going to ask for plenty more, branding and shipping and——"

"Skip it," Bart said and reined Ghost after a dodging steer.

Clouds formed in the sky as they worked.

Once Bart felt a drop of rain on his cheek and wondered how did cattle act in a storm, when they were bunched and tired?

At length, as the sun dropped over the ridge, and the clouds cleared away, and the last lingering calf went through the gate, Bart realized that the cattle had been moved.

He could hardly believe it. This morning it had seemed such an ordeal, and now it was over. He glanced around at the riders, sitting relaxed in their saddles. It was routine to them, but he had passed his first test.

"That's all for today," Frank said. "So long, Bart. So long, Danny. Don't get lost going back to Sky Camp." With John Holi Mae, and Keoki and Kim, he rode off down the trail.

Bart suddenly straightened in his saddle. His eyes met Danny's, and he realized all at once that another day had passed and that Dick might have brought Doc's letter up to camp.

Danny read his thoughts.

"Let's go," he said. "Last man there cooks supper."

The two boys raced neck and neck for a few feet, then, like good cowmen, slacked their horses to a running walk and headed for home.

But when they reached the yard, there was no Ford truck in sight. Just the golden horse Pirate with his neck over the fence, and his eyes still holding that puzzled look.

Bart slid from his saddle and opened the gate. Pirate nickered and crowded up.

"He can't savvy it," Danny said. "How much longer . . ." His voice trailed off.

"Yes, I know," Bart said. "How much longer is he going to stay like this? How much longer before he'll refuse to eat and begin to wander away?"

Bart unsaddled and put his stuff in the shed. He turned to the house to cook supper, when all at once the purr of a motor sounded.

"Doc's letter," Bart said, and resisted an impulse to run up the road toward Dick and Helen who drove toward the cabin. No, it wouldn't do to seem too anxious. He had to be careful and not show how much Doc's letters meant. They might think he wasn't happy here. He was, but Doc's letter about Pirate——

At length they came through the gate. Helen got out, and Dick. She put her arm around Bart's shoulders and mussed his hair, just like Larry used to do.

What was there about his hair? Sometimes he wished he were bald.

Dick smiled and whistled at sight of Ghost, as he fished in his pockets.

"Bart, you'd hardly know that horse," he praised.

Bart felt his heart thump. He caught sight of Doc's letter as Dick hauled it out, with Holiday Hospital in the corner and Doc's hurried scrawl. He was always in too much of a hurry to make his letters legible.

"I have some clean clothes for you, Bart. I'll put them inside," Helen said and disappeared.

Dick followed her.

Bart sank to the steps and tore the letter open with trembling hands. He pulled it out and read it, from the bottom up, fast, for news. In half a dozen sentences that stood out so that he'd never forget them, he got the idea.

Bits of words flashed at him: "Oil's no use. It won't replace the hoof, ever. They usually shoot horses like that. In the long run, it's a kindness to them."

Bart's hand squeezed the paper until it rattled. A raindrop hit him on the nose. Dimly he heard Dick say inside to Helen, "This'll end the kids having to stay up here. A good rain'll fill the tanks." Pirate came up and sniffed at the letter, then snorted.

Bart put out a hand to touch the nose of the horse. He reread part of the letter. "Send me a hoofmark and a cast. I'll have Bateman make a shoe to fit. There's always a chance."

Bart closed the letter and got inside, for by now the rain was really coming down. He held the letter out for Helen to read. But after one quick look at his face, she shoved it back.

"No, Bart, it's yours," she said, above the roar of the tropical storm.

"Doc's fine," Bart managed. "Sends his love."

"That's wonderful," Dick said. His eyes took in Bart's white face. "Tell you what, boy," he said gently. "You ride home with us in the truck. Danny'll trail the horses down tomorrow. I'll send the truck for the stuff."

Bart looked out at Pirate who limped toward the shed for shelter.

"Would you mind if I stayed and came down with Danny?" He paused a moment, then went on, "And, Dick, could you find a place to keep Pirate? Larry wants me to send him a horseshoe the size of the hoof and a cast, to show some idea of the extent of the injury. Maybe Mr. Bateman can make a shoe for him." He stopped again, then added, "Bateman's good. He's extra good. He taught me to do some shoeing. He shod Seabiscuit out in California. He's really good, really super."

Bart stopped and flushed, realizing that he was talking too much.

"Sure, bring him down," Dick said unsteadily, looking at Helen. "We'll find a place for him." He moved toward the door, shrugging off Bart's thanks. "Come on, Helen."

Bart sank to a chair and read Doc's letter again, and again and again. At last he turned to Danny and said, above the sound of frying meat, "Well, Doc lays it on the line." He jumped up to stare out of the window and down along the cement apron that funneled water into the big steel tank. "He says to drink the water and put the oil on my saddle where it'll do some good."

Danny laughed, but softly—for Danny.

"He says too," Bart went on, "that it'd be a mercy to shoot Pirate." Suddenly Bart stuffed the letter in his pocket and swung to help Danny. "But if he thinks I'll ever do that, he's crazy. Just plain crazy!"

"Sure, crazy," Danny echoed. But his voice above the sound of the rain on the roof sounded hollow.

Chapter 8

PIRATE TAKES A RUN

The next morning the rain was still coming down in torrents.

"We'll start as soon as we can saddle up," Danny said as they ate.

Bart looked his relief. He wanted to get down to that blacksmith shop.

"It's just water," Danny said, after they'd eaten and washed the dishes. He shrugged into his slicker with a wide grin. "On the Kukaiau they say that water just keeps things oiled up for more work."

Bart slipped into his own slicker that Dick had brought up for him. At the time he'd wondered why he'd need that. Now, as he let himself out the door and moved toward the barn, he was grateful for its shelter.

Pirate nickered his greeting as Bart came through the door. He walked over to nuzzle Bart's arm and sniff at the new oily smell of the yellow raincoat.

Bart bent to look at the foot which was just the same, with the torn hoof ragged and misshapen.

Danny came over too.

"Your doctor's right," he said. "It'll be tough to shoe that foot. Mr. Hunter didn't tell you. But he had a blacksmith from Honolulu come and try it. He gave up. Another man from Hilo just shook his head and wouldn't even light a fire in the forge." Danny straightened up. "What is there to nail a shoe to?"

Bart turned to get his saddle.

"Bateman's done some great things," he said. "I used to fool around his shop and watch. He let me shoe some horses too."

Bart tossed his blanket and saddle on Ghost who stood beside Pirate.

"He's so small he looks like a colt beside the big horse," Danny said as he, too, saddled up. "But he's really doing all right."

Bart cinched his saddle tight.

"While everything to do with Pirate is hitting the skids," he added. "But we'll fix that."

He led the gray outside and mounted. Pirate came into the air, shook his head, and ducked for the barn.

"Oh no you don't," Bart said and tossed his rope over the big golden horse's small head. "We've got business at Kukaiau."

He moved off, followed by Danny on his black.

"A truck'll pick up our stuff later today," Danny said.

They rode out of the gate, which Danny closed, then down the trail. Another time Bart would have enjoyed this ride through the slashing rain and watched the little rivulets make tiny rivers in the dirt of the road. He'd have laughed with Danny at the cows humped against the storm and the calves burrowed deep under the flanks of their mothers.

Now he could only sit close in his saddle and feel the dot and carry, dot and carry of Pirate's foot as the horse limped the seven miles down the trail.

At length they sighted the barn, the gray painted house, the guesthouse to the left, and clustered down the road, the small houses of the workers at the ranch.

"She looks pretty good to me," Danny said.

Bart's eyes found the little blacksmith shop off by itself.

"Me, too," he said and rode down to unsaddle his gray, check in at the house, and finally lead Pirate toward the shop.

"You'll probably need some help," Danny said and came along.

"Could be," Bart replied, and was glad for Danny's cheerful face.

They reached the shop and Bart opened the door. Pirate snorted and backed away and a fine sweat, even in the rain, made his body steam. His eyes grew green with fright.

Danny said, "His ancestor, that big stallion that kicked his way free of that ship, must have looked like that once."

Bart agreed. What a horse that must have been. But what a horse this was also. He spoke softly to Pirate and pulled on his rope.

"Come on, boy," he urged. "Come on."

Pirate reached the door, then bolted. He knocked Bart spinning and whizzed by Danny. He took the rope and left a trail right up through the woods.

Bart struggled to his feet and ran to watch. Suddenly he turned to Danny.

"Did you see that?" he demanded. "He ran without a limp."

Danny scratched his head.

"I guess so," he said, and wiped the mud from his face. "I didn't notice."

Bart ran to get the horse who'd dropped his head to graze. He brought him back and they began all over again.

"If he can take two or three steps without limping, he can take more when he gets shoes on," Bart said, and there was excitement in his voice.

"Maybe, maybe not," Danny said. "It's in the soft mud, and that's a lot different than over this volcanic stuff in dry weather."

"Sure, sure," Bart said. "But, anyway, he did it." He took hold of the big golden horse's rope and began once more to urge him into the shop.

At length, after an hour's work in the pouring rain, Pirate consented to step inside the door.

"Okay, now if you'll hold him, Danny," Bart said, and walked over to the forge. It was much like that of Mr. Bateman in Lincoln, with a hand blower and a square bank for the fire. A tub of water to temper the metal stood close by.

Bart put his hand on the anvil, smooth and cold to

the touch. A thrill went through him. Working in iron fascinated him. His hand slipped down to grasp a hammer. He hit a soft blow on the anvil and Mr. Bateman's words came to him: "You've got the touch, Bart. I could teach you——"

Mr. Bateman had taught him, too, a great deal that he was glad now that he knew. He had even let him shoe Dr. Hoak's saddle mare with light shoes. For a second Bart was tempted to put shoes on Pirate right now. His eyes ranged to the wall where a row of shoes hung on a rail. Beyond them in a rack lay the frying-pan branding irons of the Kukaiau. Big thick ones for the cattle, slender, thin ones that they used to brand the horses.

But Bart knew that Pirate wasn't ready for shoeing. He found a shoe, estimating the size, and came back to lift Pirate's injured foot.

Danny, after one look at Pirate, called, "Let's shut the door." He turned just as the big horse hit it with his head.

Pirate staggered back, fell flat on his side, then came up on all fours. His hide steamed with the heat of his body, and he trembled all over.

Bart put a hand along his neck and spoke softly to him. He took the shoe and let the horse smell it. He rubbed it along his neck, then bent again to lift his foot.

"Too large," he said, dismayed at the shrunken hoof.

Danny reached to bring him a second shoe. Bart

fitted it to the foot. But the hoof had grown long on one side.

"We'll have to trim it," Danny said.

Bart nodded and reached for the trimmers.

He worked on and on, until a gong sounded. Dinner was something to be swallowed, and he was back at it once more.

The men came in from working cattle, and still Bart hadn't gotten a shoe to fit as he'd like it to.

At length, as the dark settled over the little shop, he put Pirate's foot down.

Dick Hunter's body darkened the door still further.

Bart turned around, his face sweat-streaked, his eyes deep-socketed with fatigue.

Dick came over to take the shoe from Bart's hands. His face had the look of a man who wanted to help but couldn't find anything to do.

"It's as good as I can make it," Bart explained. "I'll draw a picture to show the damage up the side of the hoof."

Dick turned the shoe in his hands.

"We'll send it air mail," he said, gently, and helped Bart with the paper outline of the hoof.

"Sure, air mail," Bart said. "That, and I'll write Mr. Bateman. He's a wonderful blacksmith."

Bart began to straighten up the shop that Pirate had wrecked.

"I'm sorry to have messed the place up," he said.

Dick waved a hand, and Bart untied Pirate's rope

and led him from the shop. The rain had ceased and stars were coming out.

"I'm going down to Kukaiau Post Office after supper," Dick called. "I could mail your letter and the shoe. Maybe you'd like to come along?"

Bart nodded, feeling better. He knew that Dick was making the trip especially for him.

"Swell," he said, and moved on with Pirate to the barn, and then to the house to write Doc.

Chapter 9

EDIE'S MESSAGE

After supper Dick handed Bart the keys to the car.

Helen, who had gone to the kitchen, came in to look questioningly from one to the other, her hands full of covered dishes.

"We're just going down to the post office to mail a letter," Dick explained.

"Can I hire you as carriers first?" she asked.

"No!" said Dick. "Never!" He started to take the dishes from her hands, but Bart beat him to it.

"It's just some soup and things for Esther Holi Mae, who's in bed with a cold. And I thought I'd look in on the hall to see what needs fixing for the Christmas program this year. We've not even decided how Santa Claus is going to come this time."

"In May?" Dick exclaimed.

"Certainly, May. Why, Christmas will be here before we know it, and we've got to surprise the children this year."

Dick smiled. "I'll wait in the car, Mrs. Santa."

Helen and Bart walked down the road that led to the houses of the cowboys of Kukaiau.

As they passed the hall, Helen said, "We have the celebration and entertainment here. After that we serve waffles and hot cakes and coffee at our house. Larry writes that you're quite an artist with the hot cakes and waffles."

Bart smiled and shook his head. "Doc exaggerates," he said. "But I've noticed some kids around playing mouth organs. I could start a little harmonica band."

"Oh, Bart, could you? And if we could think up some way that would be different to have Santa Claus come. You see, it's the biggest secret of the year here. And we have to have him come a different way every time."

"I'll work on it," Bart promised.

They reached a little white house with green shutters, and Helen knocked on the door.

A tall Hawaiian girl of fifteen in a flowered skirt and orange-colored blouse opened the door. Her eyes were soft brown and her hair had a natural curl.

"Edie, this is Bart Holiday," Helen said.

Edie smiled and said, "Hi, Bart," then opened the door wide.

Bart stepped inside with Helen and he thought he'd never seen such a clean kitchen in his life.

"I've brought your mother some hot soup," Helen said, and handed the dish to the girl.

Edie took it and put it on the table. "She'll be so pleased. Won't you step in and say hello?"

Bart watched Edie as she moved. She was lithe and Bart thought she'd be a plenty good dancer. She was so quick and light on her feet.

"I'll be just a minute," Helen said to Bart.

Edie hung up a towel with a deft hand and turned to walk across to the window and stare out into the night. "I saw you with Pirate," she said in a soft voice. "It's wonderful that you're going to try to save him."

Bart waved his hand.

"I wish I could be sure," he said, and told her about Pirate's foot.

"You will," Edie said. "I'm sure you will, and Tasy'll be out of her head when she comes back from Hilo and finds out."

"I'd give a thousand dollars if I was as sure as you," Bart said, then grinned. "That is, if I had it to give."

"Anyway, it's wonderful—and if there's anything I can do? The men are all behind you. Dad, that's John Holi Mae, thinks you'll do it. They all want to help, but they're shy about interfering."

"Interfering!" Bart exclaimed. "I thought they'd think I was a little soft in the head."

"Oh no," Edie said. "You see, they worshiped Des, and Des would have wanted to put Pirate back on four feet more than anything."

Bart swallowed a lump as big as an apple in his throat. "Des was such a good ranch hand. He could rope and ride so well. I feel like a greenhorn."

"You needn't," Edie declared. "You'll learn."

Helen came back into the room then, and no more was said. She and Bart walked back through the dark to the big hall to turn on the light and look around. It was dusty and hardly used, except for entertainments and a big celebration July 7th, the day when Hawaii was annexed by the United States.

"One year we had Santa Claus come in as a tree," Helen said. "He was wrapped in green gauze. Another time as a side of beef all swathed in cheesecloth."

Bart looked around the big hall, with the chairs and the stage, empty now, but ready.

Helen said, "It won't be long."

"No, I guess it won't at that," Bart said, realizing all he had to do before then.

By Christmas he had to have Pirate well. He had to have him through the cattle loading and stepping proudly along on four good feet. Now he had some idea of having Santa Claus come on Pirate across the paddock.

Suddenly on the night air came the distant buzz of a plane going from Hilo to Honolulu. Bart didn't think much of it at the moment. The sound swelled, then came over and faded from their hearing.

They walked out into the dark. Helen locked the door, and they moved back along the trail to the house.

The car still stood before the door. The smell of cigar smoke drifted from it, and Dick, as they came up, switched on the lights and stepped out.

"Ready?" he asked Bart, and again handed him the keys.

"Sure! I've got the stuff right here."

"I think I'll come too," said Helen, climbing briskly into the back seat. "It's a perfect night for a drive."

"A perfect night for a drive." Bart, settled comfortably at the wheel, couldn't have agreed more. If only they could drive all night.

"I suppose you'd go to sleep at the wheel if we drove all night," said Dick suddenly, "and we'd pile up on some curve."

Thought transference! "I'll bet you a dollar I wouldn't sleep at all!" Bart retorted. "I've driven all night plenty of times with Doc, when we went to see a patient or deer hunting in the Black Hills of Dakota."

Dick turned to look over the back of the seat at Helen. "How long a drive did you have in mind?" he asked.

"Oh, something like around the island," she said airily. "If you two adventurers will take turns driving and not go to sleep at the wheel. But, if you don't mind, I think I'll take a rain check. After all, I prefer sleeping in my own bed." She got out of the car and waved as they drove away.

Bart was elated. What a chance to see some of the things Doc had talked about—Captain Cook's Kealakekua Bay, where the song "Little Grass Shack" was written, and where the great explorer had been killed by natives; the lava flow of 1950 that was still so hot you could scarcely walk on it; the Black Sands Beach on the east coast; and Volcano House on the rim of Kilauea crater.

Chapter 10

CHALLENGE RIDE

They drove down the grade that led toward Kukaiau Post Office. At the big wooden gate with the rain cover over it they stopped and Dick got out to open it, then got back in, when Bart had driven through.

They heard a rustling sound in the woods and the gentle neigh of a horse.

Dick put a hand on Bart's arm.

"Wait," he said in a half whisper.

Bart's hands tightened on the wheel. He could scarcely believe his eyes. From beneath the trees came a motley band of ragged dwarfed ponies.

"Are they real?" he whispered. His eyes followed the tiny stunted horses as they moved silently through the trees, dropping their heads at intervals to graze.

One here, another there, kicked and scampered from the trail, like truant schoolboys.

"Wild horses," Dick said. "The lack of water in the High Country drives them down."

Bart turned in his seat, his mind working fast. He

could scarcely believe that Pirate had come from such stock.

"You mean these are Pirate's blood relatives?"

Dick nodded. "Right. Any of these little mares might have been his mother."

"It's fantastic," Bart exclaimed as the horses left the road and moved from sight into the ohia trees. Nothing remained but the soft thud of tiny ragged hoofs on the native grass. "Then Pirate is really a wild palomino of Hawaii?" Bart let the car in gear and drove on down the mountainside.

"Yes." Dick nodded. "Years and years ago pirate ships sailed these waters." He paused as the car picked up speed and dropped down the grade to run along sugar plantations, then went on, "Rumor has it that a palomino stallion being shipped from Spain to California kicked free of his ship and landed here. Once ashore, he joined other horses brought here by Captain R. J. Cleveland in 1803 and fled with some of them to the wild slopes of Mauna Kea. There they had to fight for a livelihood." Dick sighed. "They're going fast. It's only a question of time, with the wild dogs pulling them down and the drought killing them by thirst."

"It's tough," Bart said and still could scarcely credit what he'd seen: the little horses with tiny faces peeking out from behind long matted manes, their ragged bodies filing through the ghostly trees.

They drove on to stop at Kukaiau to drop the parcel in the post office, then raced north along a highway that skirted the sea. The name Paauilo flashed on a signboard. Bart caught sight of a huge steel structure off to the right and down by the water.

"That's Robbie's sugar mill," Dick said. "We'll visit him soon."

Bart nodded and pressed harder on the accelerator.

It seemed then that the Ford station wagon almost took wings as they sped northward, past Honokaa, then swung west at Paauhau, leaving the sugar fields behind to ride across open grasslands dotted with cactus.

They swept past a low set of buildings sprawled across the flatlands at Kamuela.

"The Parker ranch," Dick explained. "Second largest ranch under the American flag. Over to the right is Kawaihae where we'll load cattle. Getting sleepy?" he asked cautiously.

"Nope, I'm not sleepy," Bart said, and pushed the car harder.

They drove south through old lava flows, the car gliding between beds of black lava and grass that glistened yellow under the moonlight.

"The flows of the eighteen hundreds," Dick explained with a wave of his hand toward Mauna Kea towering snow-capped to the left. "That was when she was active."

Bart nodded.

They reached Kailua and suddenly began to climb. After half an hour they reached Keokea Junction and pulled over to the side of the road, then got out to stretch.

Beneath them lay the little round palm-fringed bay.

"Kealakekua," Dick said, and pointed to a little white monument along the shore. "Captain Cook's," he added. "He was killed right there by native Hawaiians in 1779."

"I know, Doc told me," Bart said.

As they came back to the car Bart looked at Dick before he got behind the wheel. He felt as though he'd never be sleepy again as long as he lived, but still——

"Maybe I'd better drive. Helen might be watching." Dick grinned and slid behind the wheel. "I'll drive to the Black Sands; it's something under a hundred miles."

"Okay." Bart got in and the car started, to climb steadily through tiny coffee plantations that lay on both sides of the road. Off to the left Mauna Loa, still active, still erupting on an average of every five years, towered above them.

After a few miles Dick stopped the car amid a scarred lava-laden area and got out.

"Want to see something of this?" he asked, and led the way up the slope over black lava formation that had cooled in grotesque formations. At length he paused to stoop and take a chunk of it in his hand, then pass it to Bart.

"Still hot," Bart exclaimed, juggling the rock to keep from getting burned.

"After three years." Dick nodded and led the way to a thermometer close by. By the light of a match he struck Bart read, "Two thousand degrees. Whew!" He studied the rod that sank down into the hot lava bed.

"After three years of cooling off?" Dick queried. "How

hot do you think it was when it came flowing down the mountain?"

Bart shook his head and grinned as they turned back to the car.

As they drove on, Bart got out his harmonica and began to play. The car wheels hummed along. The sky was blue ink as they wound through scrub wild gooseberry. Once a herd of wild pigs crossed the road, the old boar turning to charge the car with sharp guttural grunts.

Dick smiled and Bart laughed aloud.

"They're fast," Dick said. "If you ever get near them be careful. Remember, you can outrun them uphill, but downhill you don't have a chance. An old boar could rip your leg wide open with his tusks."

"Up or down, I'll give them a wide berth," Bart promised. He lay back in his seat and began to play some old square-dance melodies.

The car droned along.

Suddenly Bart stifled a yawn, another. His harmonica sagged in his hand. . . .

Two hours later the motion of the car stopping brought him awake. He sat up and looked at the sea before him, and the ragged coast line, then reddened.

"Guess I lose," he said with a grin, and reached into his pocket, then silently handed Dick a silver dollar.

Bart looked out through the windshield. A small streak of light showed in the east, but the sand beneath them was black as night.

"This is the famous Black Sands Beach," Dick explained. "Lava formation that, through centuries of erosion and weathering, has become sand."

They got out to walk down to the shore, then along the sand that lay along the sloping shore. At length they came back to the car.

"Next stop, Kilauea Volcano House," Dick said.

"And the crater," Bart exclaimed. Doc had told him plenty about the huge caldron-like circular lava pit that was seven hundred and fifty feet deep and over three thousand feet across. "Let's get going," he said.

At the car Bart waited.

Dick got on the left and Bart slid happily behind the wheel. "What a guy! What a guy," he told himself as he started the motor and swung the car toward the highway. "And what a car, brother!"

They moved off and again the car seemed to take to the air. They headed north along a winding road, and Bart kept up a steady stream of talk. Suddenly he said, "Look at those trees over there, Dick!" There was no answer. Bart sneaked a look at his front-seat passenger and laughed softly.

Dick lay stretched out in the seat and his breath came even and regular.

Again the motion of the car as it turned into the rustic wood-brown Volcano House did the trick.

Dick sat up and faced Bart, then burst into a loud laugh. "Okay, okay, now we're even." He fished out the dollar and handed it back to Bart.

"We're still not home yet," warned Bart.

They stopped before the two-story wooden building and walked inside. The smell of hot coffee hit them.

"Brother!" Dick exclaimed and made for the counter. Bart followed.

They ate hot cakes and bacon and eggs, then moved out to the balcony and stood breathless as the east lightened. A wide expanse of trees in the foreground met their eyes. To the right, and perhaps a mile away, tiny smoke plumes filtered from the rough ground. Straight ahead, and perhaps two miles distant, lay the scarred area that bordered the crater of Kilauea.

Then suddenly the sun came up, and the pink dawn tinted the whole landscape.

"Come on," Dick said. "We'll take in the crater."

Bart guided the car along the narrow road over scarred ground barren of vegetation.

"The gases and ash kill the vegetation," Dick explained, as they drove on to stop at a parking area, then got out to walk over black lava and white pumice stones and toward a sign that said, "Crater Rim. Caution!"

Then suddenly they reached the edge and stared hundreds of feet straight down over a ragged rock rim into the crater itself.

"Whew!" Bart drew in his breath. "Look at that cone." His eyes focused on a flat black seething area dotted with cinder-cone humps that boiled and bubbled and exploded lava high into the air.

"Some sight," Dick agreed. "You should have seen it

when the lava over the whole crater was fire-red and churning."

"I sure wish I had," Bart said enviously, as he read the small print on the sign: "People approach the rim at their own peril." "Anybody ever go over?" he asked.

"One man last year," Dick said. "A suicide, they think."

After half an hour they turned back to the car.

"Now for Hilo," Dick said, and got behind the wheel.

Bart climbed in and they drove on down past Volcano House and toward Hilo. As the car hummed along Bart tried to recall what Doc had said about Hilo. There was something Doc had said he should see there. But what was it?

Bart looked on both sides of the road. Trees, fern trees, and fuchsias grew in a perfect forest as far as the eye could see.

"Flowers, flowers, flowers," Bart told himself but could get no clue. It wasn't until they got to Hilo and were driving down the main street that Bart finally percolated. A sign caught his eyes that said, "Flowers of Hawaii." An arrow pointed to the right. "Of course!" he said, then added shyly, "Dick, do you suppose we could go down to Orchids of Hawaii? I've always had a yen to see their greenhouses."

Dick's answer was to swing the car sharp right and follow the sign. In ten minutes they drew up to the entrance.

"Eight o'clock," he said. "They should open up any minute."

Bart had a sudden brain wave. He slipped from the car and said, "You've seen this layout a hundred times, Dick. How's about me going through alone?"

Dick looked closely at him, then smiled.

"Why not?" he said, and leaned back with a yawn.

"See you," Bart said, and moved inside to stand in a fairyland of blooms. There were rooms and rooms full of huge gorgeous flowers. Rows and rows of pots that thrust beautiful flowers up into the hot steamy air of the greenhouse.

Bart stood there and suddenly said, "I wonder, Mom, what you'd like?" He closed his mouth and looked around to make sure no one had heard.

Then a salesgirl came up, just as Bart spotted what he wanted, a huge orchid and white flower, that would be exactly right with Helen's dark coloring.

"Wrapped as a gift?" the girl asked as he paid her.

Bart nodded. A gift, of course, repaying some of what she'd already given him. He waited amid the flowers, then took the wrapped parcel and walked back to the car.

Again Bart realized how swell Dick was. No questions from him as he put the parcel in the back. Just a grin as Bart again climbed behind the wheel, and a wave of his arm north as the car wound through Hilo and hit the highway.

They reached the turnoff at Kukaiau in the middle of the morning and drove up through the cane fields once more. The sun lay warm on the hills and glistened on the smooth blue sea.

At the big wooden gate Bart said, "I'll get it. You opened it before."

Bart sprang to open the gate and Dick drove through. They pushed on until they reached a bit of ground almost covered with bracken. Dick stopped the car and got out to take some of it in his hands, as Bart came up to him.

"It's choking the grass all over the island," he said with a worried crease between his eyes. "We've got to work out some way to reseed."

Bart recalled the plane he'd heard go over the ranch as he'd stood with Helen. He bent down to examine the ground, and as he did some seeds from a high grass plant shelled to the fallow earth. Idly he watched them fall and disappear into the bracken. Suddenly he said, "Has any seeding by airplane ever been tried?"

Dick looked quickly around, and his eyes widened with a pleased look of appreciation.

"Why, no, Bart," he said. "I don't believe so, and it might work. It just might." He broke off with a smile. "Well, we'd better get on. Helen'll be waiting."

They drove up the road and to the ranch. Helen came out of the house.

"Who won the money?" Helen asked.

Bart retrieved the parcel from the back seat, then got out to face Dick. They both grinned at one another, then at her.

"I see," she said with a smile. "It was a draw."

Bart held out the box.

"For you," he said awkwardly.

They stood there as Helen undid the flower. Bart saw her lips tremble and wished he'd thrown himself in the crater. Des must have given her one once and he had reminded her of it. Bart gulped and turned away.

But Helen pulled him gently around to face her.

"It's lovely," she said. "I'm so touched, Bart, dear. Thank you." She reached up and kissed him.

Chapter 11

THE ROPING LESSON

It seemed to Bart that the following days crowded by like cattle going through a chute.

He worked with Ghost and his roping and kept up the water on Pirate's foot.

"It won't do any harm," he told Danny. "It keeps it clean."

A week passed, then another, and each day brought the time closer to when he'd get the package from Doc with the shoe from Bateman.

He practiced his roping with Ghost and Frank Correia helped him. They rode down to the Corn Field paddock one day.

"You've been doing pretty well with moving cattle," Frank said. "So today we'll go into the matter of roping calves in the open."

"I'm not much good at roping so far." Bart's voice was discouraged.

Frank dismounted as they neared a bunch of cows with their calves.

"First you see that your saddle cinch is right. Not too tight, but just right." He let Bart run his hand under the cinch of his roan. "The calves are pretty husky and you wouldn't want your saddle to turn."

Bart turned from the roan.

"They're husky all right. It's just four more days until branding time. If that stuff doesn't come for Pirate so I can use him, I don't know what I'll do. Use Ghost I guess."

"You could do worse," Frank said. "Of course, he's too green to work in the corral yet, but we'll give you another horse."

"Yes," Bart thought, and his pulse leaped. "Pirate."

He got on Ghost and made a loop in his rope as Frank showed him, and they rode toward the calves.

"There's one about your size," Frank said. "Toss your rope on him."

Bart touched Ghost with his boots and the little horse spurted ahead.

The calf ran down the hill. Bart reached him with his loop swinging over his head and made his throw. The calf turned sharply to the left and Ghost and Bart sailed on by.

Frank did not smile at Bart's red face.

"It happens to the best of us," he said. "Ghost is as green as you. But you'll learn together."

"It wouldn't happen if I were on Pirate," Bart decided.

"Try again," Frank said.

Bart tried again and again and again. He pulled up and let his eyes go out to the trees filled with red ohia blooms. He got off to pat the little gray horse's lathered neck, then tried his saddle cinch.

"It's loose," he said.

Frank smiled. "The little guy is learning fast," he said. "Watch him, and when he isn't looking, tighten your cinch. You see, a saddle horse learns to take a deep breath and hold it when you cinch them up. That way they don't get caught with a tight girth."

"Okay," Bart said. "Let's try again."

Frank worked with Bart until the sun stood overhead. They dropped from their horses, unbridled them to graze, then ate their sandwiches.

"Four days from now and this place'll be a madhouse," Frank said as he lay back and stared up at the blue sky. "This cattle branding is a big event. One year we had Millard Sheets, the artist, here. He sent us Sturdy Defense from the mainland, you know. The sire of all these horses. He got a great kick out of branding. Pretty good with a rope too." Frank took a bite out of a beef sandwich and went on. "The Honolulu paper sends a man to report it too."

"I'll have to stay away from him," Bart said ruefully. "I can see the headline now: GREENHORN ROPES SELF IN RECORD TIME!"

"Oh, I don't know," Frank said. "I wasn't so good at first either. But that's another story." He got up and started toward his big roan.

Bart rebridled Ghost and they rode once more toward the herd.

Bart worked then until the sweat stood out under his new hat. He got his rope on a calf. The calf circled him and tied Ghost in a knot. The little horse began to buck and sent Bart rolling across the grass, then ran into the woods.

The calf ran back to its mother, trailing Bart's new rope.

Frank brought Ghost back, then raced to retrieve Bart's rope.

"Tell you what," he said. "Maybe we've been rushing this business? Let's run a few cows and calves into the corral and work from there. It's more the way we'll work anyway when we brand."

A line came out along Bart's mouth.

"No, we'll work right here," he said, then added, "Sorry, Frank. I mean, I'd rather get the hang of this thing right now."

Frank put a hand along the tree of his saddle.

"Sure, Bart, sure thing, if that's the way you want it."

Bart could tell that he was pleased. Bart made a loop in his rope. He was glad Pirate wasn't around to see how awkward he was as he rode down to the same calf.

"Okay, guy," he said. "We'll take that again."

He put the gray horse after the calf. He leaned low in the saddle and finally dropped the loop on the calf.

The calf ran under Ghost's belly. The rope tightened

and the gray began to buck. Only this time Bart landed on a cinder cone and lay still.

When he came to, Frank was bent over him. Bart fought to a sitting position, then to his feet. Two lines ran between his eyes and his jaw was set.

Frank said afterward to the men, "It seemed as though his hair caught fire, though of course it could have been the sun through the trees."

In silence Bart walked to pick up his hat, then took the rope that Frank again retrieved from the calf.

"Now!" he said, and mounted Ghost for the third time. He put the little horse after the same calf.

"Oh, you want it again?" the calf seemed to say, and ran bawling up the hill.

Bart put the Ghost after the calf. In the last two hours the horse had learned a great deal, as had Bart. The boy felt the Ghost give under him, felt his sudden grasp of what was wanted, as they raced along.

Bart leaned down and dropped his rope over the calf's head and pulled the gray to a halt. The calf ran the length of the rope and spun around, then began to circle.

But the gray had wised up. He kept turning to keep his head toward the calf.

Bart dismounted and ran down the rope to gather the bawling, kicking calf in his arms and flip him to the soft ground. He sat on the squirming calf for a moment, then flipped off his rope and stood up.

The calf ran back to its mother and Bart walked back toward Ghost, coiling his rope as he went.

"You'll do, Bart," Frank said. "Take it from there."

Bart nodded. It was just getting dusk. He mounted Ghost and rode with Frank back to the ranch, tired but satisfied. As he rode into the yard, the car stood before the door, and beside it stood a tall girl with a pointed chin, blond hair, and laughing blue eyes. Helen said, "Bart, this is Anastasia."

"Hello, Tasy—I'll have to call you that. It fits so well," Bart said. He'd have gone on, but there stood Dick with a parcel.

It had Doc's scrawl on it, Bart could see as Dick, his eyes bright, held it out. And it was big enough for a shoe for Pirate.

For a second Bart's hand hesitated. He could hardly believe that it was finally here, that within this parcel lay the means of getting Pirate back to ranch life. Really to life itself, for without work the horse would surely go to pieces.

"You'll have to excuse Bart, Tasy," Dick explained. "He's working on a shoe for Pirate and this is it." He put the parcel into Bart's hands.

"Dinner's in half an hour," Helen said tactfully, above Tasy's exclamation of pleasure. "And we'll have to get busy on the *leis* for the cattle drive. Come on, Tasy. You'll have to unpack, and, Dick, perhaps you'll bring that bag inside?"

Bart took the box from Dick, grateful to them all. He walked down to the blacksmith shop and inside and switched on the light, then sat on an upturned box to open the parcel.

He was aware that Danny came in as he lifted out the shoe. All in one quick glance he saw that it was a wonderful job and built up on one side.

"Looks fine," he said.

Danny took the shoe. "Yes," he said. "But we can only tell when we try it on."

Bart nodded, already opening Doc's letter that was stuffed inside the package.

"Dear Bart," it began. "Well, here it is. Bill Bateman says it's the best he can do and not to expect miracles. That with a hoof like that, the best thing to do would be to turn the horse out to graze and skip it. But, if I know you—and I should after seventeen years—you'll want to put the shoe on, rather than sit reading a lot of advice you won't follow."

There was more, lots more, about the shop and the hospital and his work and a little item about him perhaps going around the world for the government. "Maybe coming back by Hawaii next summer, in June. About roundup time if I remember."

Bart folded the letter and put it safely in the upper pocket of his shirt.

A supper gong sounded, and Bart stood up to walk to the door.

"We'd better wait until morning to shoe Pirate," he said.

Danny nodded. "Yes, we'll need all the light we can get."

"Then we'll try him out."

"Yes," Danny said. "The next day's the roundup."

Bart took the precious shoe and walked toward the door. Dick would want to see it, and after supper he'd go down and try it on Pirate just for size.

"Yes," Bart said. "And Pirate's got to be in it."

"Sure," Danny said. "Sure thing." He didn't look as if he meant it. "I suppose the horse'll have time to get used to it as we work—if we take him slow?"

Bart gave Danny a quick look, then started to walk toward the house.

"I think so," he said. "His shoe'll settle to the foot, if we take him easy," and he walked on.

Chapter 12

FALSE SHOE

Bart led Pirate across to the shop the next morning as the birds sleepily wakened in the ohia trees.

But early as he was, Danny was there ahead of him, with a fire glowing in the forge, the shoeing platform swept off, and fresh water in the tempering tub.

Bart led Pirate up to the shop door and expected a struggle. But the horse moved inside and over to the platform as though he'd done it all his life.

Bart walked over to the forge. The smell of the smoke and the glow of the fire brought back memories of Bill Bateman's shop in Lincoln, Nebraska.

He took up a hammer and struck the anvil a soft blow. Suddenly, with that motion he had but one idea: to get the shoes on Pirate and ride him out across the rocky field.

"We'd better shoe the other three feet first," he said.

Danny hesitated, then nodded. "That's right. They all have to go on anyway, for the test."

Bart took the hoof trimmers and walked over to Pirate. He let him smell them, then ran a hand down his front foot to tap it gently with his palm.

"Up," he said, "up, Pirate," and lifted on his fetlock.

Obediently the gold horse raised his forefoot.

Slowly then, with infinite care, Bart trimmed his left front forefoot. The trimming done, he took the rasp, first the heavy one, then the lighter one, and made a perfect seat for the shoe.

Danny's eyes widened at Bart's skill.

"I can see you've done this before."

"Mr. Bateman taught me," Bart said, and shook the perspiration from his forehead. "He's the best."

He moved back to tap one of Pirate's hind feet.

Again, obedient to "Up, Pirate," the big horse let Bart lift his foot and rasp off the hoof.

It was hot, hard work.

"Let me take one," Danny said, and moved to pick up Pirate's other hind foot. A moment later he picked himself up where Pirate had flung him and walked back to the forge. "I guess he's a one-man horse," he said ruefully.

Bart took a drink of water from a jug and nodded.

"Let's hope he's at least a one-man until I get these shoes on him," he said, and bent to his work.

At length three were done. There remained but the injured foot to do.

Bart moved up front to tap Pirate's leg.

"Up, Pirate," he said gently. "Up, boy."

The horse sniffed at Bart's wet shirt and obediently lifted his foot. He seemed to sense what Bart was trying to do.

For a moment, as Bart stared down at the hoof, his heart failed him.

Danny came close to look too.

"It's a full size smaller," he said. "What are you going to nail the shoe to on that one side?"

Bart put the hoof between his knees and took up the rasp.

"We'll cross that bridge when we get the shoe ready," he said.

He worked doggedly at shaping the hoof, purposely blind to the small dwarfed foot with the outside quarter torn away and the frog all but gone entirely. At length he put the foot down and straightened up.

"Oh, my aching back," he said, and moved to the forge.

"Now for the real work," Danny said, and built up the fire.

Bart selected a shoe and walked over to pick up Pirate's good front foot.

"Right," he said, and brought the shoe back to bury it deep in the fire. While it heated, he tried two more shoes for the back feet. At length, with tongs, he took the shoe from the fire.

It glowed white hot.

Bart lifted it to the anvil and beat it out to a circle,

then walked over to test it on Pirate. He laid it on the hoof, and a strong acrid smell of scorching bone filtered through the shop and out the door.

"Ugh!" a voice said as the shop entrance darkened.

Bart glanced around and grinned.

"Come in, Tasy," he said. "But not too close."

He took the shoe back, reheated it, then reshaped it to the hoof. Twice he did this, then plunged the shoe deep in the water to temper it. The same process he repeated with the rear shoes.

At length he said, "Now, we'll nail them on."

"After lunch," Tasy said. "I was sent to tell you."

"Already?" Bart exclaimed in dismay. There was so much to do and the day was half gone. Night would fall and he wouldn't be ready. "After lunch then, Danny," he said reluctantly.

Danny nodded. "I'll throw Pirate some hay and give him a bucket of water," he said.

Bart moved with Tasy toward the house. He could tell as they walked along the road between the machine shed and the water tower that she'd done this many times before with Des.

She scarcely spoke but kept her eyes straight ahead.

"It's so wonderful to have you here," she burst out. Impulsively she put a hand along his arm. "I hope you stay—for—e—v—er—er!"

Bart gulped.

"Stay?" He'd almost forgotten that he might not, that he hadn't been here always. He opened his mouth to say something of the sort, but they'd reached the porch steps and Tasy had bolted inside.

Bart paused a moment. But would he want to stay if anything happened to Pirate? He wondered, then walked inside.

At one o'clock he came back to the shop.

Danny was already there beside the little shoeing rack that contained the horseshoe nails, the rasps, the small-headed shoeing hammer, and the pincers for cutting off the nails just above the hoof.

Bart took it over to stand it beside Pirate.

The big horse smelled of it, then nosed Bart's blue shirt. He was restive from standing so long and inclined to jump at the slightest noise.

Bart put a hand along his muscled neck.

"I'll make it as fast as I can," he promised, and bent to take up the first shoe.

It went on in jig time, as did the two rear ones. Bart nailed them to the hoofs, then snipped off the nails and rasped a space below them to clinch the nail ends.

Danny scratched his head. "Nice work," he said.

Bart barely heard him. He couldn't keep from thinking of that last shoe and where he'd nail it. At length three shoes were on.

Pirate stood with his three black hoofs shining.

Bart wiped the moisture from his forehead and took a deep drink of water. The sun lay in the west. Long shadows already crept across the lawn toward the house.

Bart picked up the fourth shoe, small and ill-shaped. All these last weeks of effort and anxiety lay bunched there in this piece of metal. It made Bart almost sick to look at it and the hoof to which it would have to be nailed.

Danny shook his head.

"Some job," he said. "To make it stick."

"Yes, some job," Bart said, and lifted Pirate's foot to place the shoe on the hoof. After studying it intently, he took it to the forge and plunged it well down into the coals. When it was hot he worked it as he had done the others.

"I don't know," Danny said as he studied the fit of the shoe on the hoof. "There's a lot of daylight there. Maybe rocks will work in?"

Bart picked up the hammer. But with the first blow of the metal on his foot, the big horse reared back. With a mighty heave he broke his rope, swerved toward the door, and with the shoe spinning across the shop, sped for the paddock.

Bart watched the horse run a few hundred feet, then stop to graze, his rope trailing. "It's tender," he said, and studied his torn pants leg, and blood oozing from a small cut made when Pirate wrenched free. "I should have figured on that."

Danny agreed. "If it's that tender, what will it be like on those rocks?"

Bart stared at Danny a moment, then walked out to coax the big horse back into the shop—to talk soothingly to him, to finally get the shoe nailed on by using small taps of the hammer.

At length he dropped the foot to the floor.

"Finished," he said.

Danny nodded. "I'll go get the saddle," he said.

Bart said, "All right," and took another drink of water. The sun had gone. The shadows lengthened. He wiped his hand across a damp forehead, and the doorway darkened once more and there stood Homer, down for the cattle drive.

He came inside, his dark eyes on Pirate's foot.

"Brother, am I tired," he said. "I've just been chief nurse to six little nene geese who've hatched out up by Lehu corral." He dropped to sit on the anvil. "A shoe?" he went on, with a nod at Pirate's shod foot.

"Bill Bateman's from Lincoln, Nebraska," Bart explained. "I'm waiting now for Danny to bring the saddle to try it out."

Homer said, "I'll ride with you, if I'm not in the way?"

Bart shook his head and turned to Danny with the saddle. In minutes he'd saddled up and led Pirate out to the yard. As he took the reins to mount, he paused a moment. His pulse pounded in spite of himself, now that the moment of the test had come.

He put a foot in the stirrup and mounted, then spoke to the big horse. Together with Homer he rode up along the hill, through Corn Field over smooth grass, and Bart felt the flow of power beneath him. After Ghost's small barrel, this was a mighty horse. He still limped some, but it was habit, and not being used to the shoes, Bart knew.

After half a mile they turned back to the ranch.

"It's getting dark now," Bart said. "Anyway, I can't really tell until we get up in the High Country."

"Yes," Homer said. "Among the cinders and rocks and pumice."

Chapter 13

THE CATTLE DRIVE

Hawaiian daylight seeped through the windows to waken Bart next morning. For a moment he lay quietly, listening to the ranch waking up.

First, there was the strident crow of a rooster down the road, then an answering one closer at hand. Lights showed, doors slammed, and women's voices came to him. All busily preparing *leis* for their men's hatbands.

Wolf pushed the back door open and moved outside, to stretch and yawn, then give a long defiant bark toward the distant cry of wild dogs far up Mauna Kea.

From far up the paddock came the thud of horses' hoofs, as Danny brought in the saddle horses for the day.

Bart sprang from bed to walk over to the window and peer out. Homer followed him to watch Dick's big bay, Helen's sorrel mare, Tasy's dark chestnut, Frank's big roan, and all the others come swinging down the slope.

"Boy! Boy!" Bart drew in his breath.

"Some sight," Homer said. "Look at Pirate lead the bunch."

Bart nodded as his eyes moved over Pirate." Yes, look at him," he said.

Bart raced into his clothes along with Homer and they moved out of the door and toward the barn.

Helen passed Bart in the hallway, her hands full of ginger and *maile leis*.

"Breakfast's in half an hour," she said, and slipped a *lei* on his hatband. "Just for size," she said. "No, you don't get to wear it until we start."

Bart nodded.

Tasy came from the bedroom, yawning. "Why do the cows get up so early? Can't we have the drive this afternoon?" she complained.

Bart grinned and pulled her hair. Already she was beginning to seem like a sister to him and this house to seem like his home. For a moment he thought of Doc. What if he could see him now with a hatband of flowers?

Bart moved out of the door and toward the barn with Homer beside him. He took a deep breath and let it out. He wanted to shout, but he closed his mouth and walked slowly along.

"You know, Homer," he said. "I feel as though I'd been here always." His eyes moved up along the paddock to estimate the number of cows that grazed there and think of the number more scattered up through the hills. "They're spread out for seven miles," he told Homer. "We'll bring them down to the corrals and have three days of branding."

"Yes," Homer said. "But I'll have to get back after the drive."

"Too bad!" Bart moved on.

He walked through the barn to the saddling shed and his locker. He took the rope Manuel had made him and brought Pirate from the corral. Suddenly in the doorway stood Manuel. In his hands he held a brand-new saddle which he held out to Bart.

Bart stared at it, unable to comprehend.

Homer nudged him. "It's for you."

"For me?"

Manuel's brown hands pushed the saddle forward. "Yes, for you, Bart, and for Pirate."

Bart knew then, as the palomino thrust his nose forward to sniff at the new leather, that it was Manuel's way of saying, "I know he's going to make it fine."

Bart couldn't speak for a minute. Finally he croaked out, "Manuel, that's a wonderful saddle. Pirate and I thank you."

Frank came over to finger the saddle. John Holi Mae ran a big brown hand across the cantle.

"You boys," Bart said. "I don't suppose you ever saw this before."

They all grinned and smiled sheepishly.

"Only all the time Manuel worked on it," John's deep voice said.

They all laughed.

Suddenly the sun popped over the mountain. It shone through the fog and lifted it. It seemed to be the signal for action.

Bart groomed Pirate's back. He put on the Navaho blanket, then hoisted the saddle to cinch it.

"The stirrups are just right," he said as he mounted.

"Well, Manuel could tell from your old saddle, you know," Homer said as he saddled his own sorrel.

"Will I ever learn?" Bart sighed.

Suddenly a gong sounded.

"Breakfast," Bart said, and raced for the house with Homer right behind.

The meal was something to be choked down. Only Helen and Dick remained calm. The reporter, who had a tiny mustache and wore riding breeches, made notes and asked a thousand questions.

But finally, they all walked outside and toward the barn.

As if by magic, from the doorways of the houses came women and girls with *leis* in their hands. They walked to the corral and to their men.

Edie Holi Mae nodded and said hello to him as she and her slim dark mother went to put a garland of flowers in John Holi Mae's hatband.

Tasy came over to Bart with a *lei* of ginger flowers.

"For you," she said, and kissed him.

For a moment Bart didn't know what to do. "Thank her, dope," Doc's voice came as clear as if his long gangling body in a white operating gown stood there beside them.

"Sure, sure, this is great, dope," Bart stammered. "I, I mean Tasy. Thanks."

Tasy laughed and walked on to take her horse and let John Holi Mae help her into the saddle.

Helen decorated Frank's hat with a blue hydrangea *lei*. Then Dick helped Helen mount before getting on his own sorrel.

He looked at Bart and said, "Take it easy, just for today. If a cow cuts back, let her go."

"Yes," Frank added as he mounted his roan. "Until we see if the shoe's going to hold. One quick false move and he could tear it right off his hoof."

Bart got into his saddle. It felt new and stiff, but it would get broken in. He took up his reins and they all started up through the trees.

The fog had lifted now, and the ohia trees, laden with their red lehua or rain-flower blooms, were all along the trail.

Bart didn't think he'd ever forget this ride to the top.

They rode double file, laughing and joking and yet with the business at hand very much in the foreground.

The reporter had trouble with his bay horse. He held the reins too tight, and the horse reared. He held them too loosely, and the horse veered off into the woods.

"Frank'll straighten him out," Homer said, as he glanced left to the corrals through which thousands of bawling calves would go in the process of being branded and marked for the Kukaiau.

They moved on up the mountain. Bright-colored scarlet birds fluttered around their horses' heads as they rode.

"They're iiwis," Homer explained. "The natives used to make royal robes of their feathers."

Through the trees, first the ohia, then as they climbed, the koa, cattle raised their head to stare as they passed.

Pirate's limp stayed with him.

"It's natural," Homer said. "He's limped a long time."

"Sure," Bart said. But a little later he rode off the trail and got off to lift the foot and examine it. "It's nothing," he added as he took his knife to dig gravel and grass from beneath the side of the shoe.

At length they reached the top.

"Nine o'clock," Homer said as Frank rode toward them. "We've made good time."

Bart agreed as Frank came close and said, "You two follow the trail back. Keep the cattle moving and a rider in sight on either side of you." To Bart he explained, "By sticking to the trail there'll be less gravel and rough cinders just for today."

Bart nodded and reined Pirate off to the left of the trail perhaps a hundred feet.

All the riders then spread out across the division fence and at a signal from Frank began to move the cattle down the mountainside.

At first there were only a few cattle. The line moved fast. Shouts echoed across the woods at intervals. It was their way of keeping in touch with one another and preventing cattle from being missed or left behind.

At length the cattle increased. Lines of bellowing Herefords became a giant red stream that flowed on and on down the slope.

The sun stood overhead, then dipped toward the west.

Bart rode Pirate steadily behind his part of the herd.

"Halfway," Homer finally said, and nodded to a group of ohia trees. "We've left the koas behind us."

Bart nodded and moved his hand down along Pirate's thick muscled neck.

They moved on and on. The stream thickened now. It became a milling giant of moving white-faced cows and bawling scurrying calves.

At last they were almost there. Ahead loomed the gates.

"Easy, don't crowd them," Frank cautioned.

Cattle now began to break for the hills. A calf here, a young cow there broke away to be hotly pursued and brought back by a rider.

Bart kept a tight rein on Pirate. He'd been very careful all day not to let him pivot on his legs too fast. Suddenly a young cow with a calf beside her fled for the woods.

"Let her go," Frank called sharply.

Bart nodded and pulled on Pirate's reins.

But the big horse, held in check all day, could take no more. A trained cow horse, he swung around and with half a dozen mighty bounds overtook the cow and brought her back into the herd, tail flying and calf bellowing in panic.

Bart followed the cow and calf to the gate that Homer closed on them, then dropped to the ground for a look at Pirate's shoe.

It seemed to be all right. He took his knife and lifted the hoof to dig around it.

"So far so good," he said, and dropped the foot back to the ground.

A murmur of relief ran around the group.

Bart led Pirate toward the barn along with Dick and Danny and Frank. He let his hand slide down along the big stallion's neck and reached to take down his rope. Two thousand calves were here to be branded with the frying-pan iron and earmarked with a half crop in the right ear within the next three days.

"So far so good," he repeated and could hardly wait for the morning's branding to begin.

Chapter 14

THE BRANDING

Bart led Pirate over to the side of the corral next morning. The Honolulu reporter had dismounted and stood outside the corral beside the branding fire that already sent a fine smoke into the hills.

There would be a few minutes respite before the branding would begin. Four sets of heavy frying-pan irons that lay buried side by side in the deep live coals had to reach white heat.

Frank moved over to take a deep drink of water from a jug. Bart followed. He tipped the vessel to let the cold water run down his throat. But his hands shook and it ran down his shirt front instead.

Danny rode over, threw himself off his horse, and took the jug from Bart.

"I know," he said. "I felt that way, too, my first branding." He tipped the jug up, then down, and wiped his lips. "Just take it easy," he begged, with a twinkle in his brown eyes. "If you catch all the calves, we'll lose our jobs. Leave a few for us."

"All right. All right," Bart said and tried to grin. He

looked off into the trees, then back to Pirate, the trained roping horse.

"Sure, he's fast," Danny said. "And you're not so slow yourself. Not with the teachers you've had: Frank and, of course, me. And Pirate's shoe is still intact, isn't it?"

Bart agreed.

"Then take it easy," Danny said.

Bart nodded, then took another drink and walked back to his horse.

Frank moved over to tighten his saddle girth. Danny, too, eased a finger beneath his own saddle cinch and decided it was fine.

Bart tested his own. It felt tight enough.

"Better give it another notch," Danny advised.

Bart pulled the latigo to the next hole and fastened the latigo strap back in its holder.

The fire glowed red now, and the irons were ready.

John Holi Mae and two other men waited to do the branding. Kim and the Hawaiian and two other cowboys stood beside the fire and waited to throw the first calf to be dragged to the corral just inside the fire location.

Frank slipped into his saddle and reached for his rope. Danny also took down his and, with a wide grin of encouragement to Bart, made a loop.

Bart remounted and began to make a loop also. His hands felt as though they had mittens on them.

"The first calf is always the hardest," Danny said and nodded toward the milling herd. "Jump in, Bart."

"Not me," Bart said. "I'll follow you boys."

Then the branding started in the way everything was done on the Kukaiau. There was no fuss. Frank just pushed his roan forward, dropped his loop on a calf's hind foot, and swung toward the fire. It was as easy as that.

Danny dropped his loop. His horse had already swerved toward the blaze.

Bart touched Pirate's side with his boots. He felt the big horse move forward at a brisk walk. With a limp to be sure, but with eyes shining and nostrils distended.

Bart reached the herd. A calf stood there. Bart would have bet it was the same calf that had fooled him out in the paddock. Pirate pressed in close to put Bart in position for the throw.

Bart took a quick dab with his loop down at the moving hind foot of the calf. The foot was in it. Bart gave the rope a quick jerk and took his dallies around the saddle horn.

"Now," he said. But already Pirate was on the way to the branding fire, dragging the bawling calf after him.

"See, it wasn't so hard, was it?" Danny breathed, as he passed Bart with his second calf.

Bart inclined his head. He reached the fire and Pirate paused. Kim and another man took charge of the calf. A second more and Bart's loop was freed of the calf's leg and swung toward him in the air.

Bart glanced around. No one was watching. It was all taken as a matter of course. He'd caught his first calf with his new rope and on Pirate! But everyone took it as though he'd caught calves all his life.

Bart wanted to shout. But he kept silent and rushed to make a second loop, for already Pirate had him close to the herd and paused impatiently, as much as to say, "Well, what are we waiting for?"

Bart fashioned his second loop and dropped it on a second calf. The work went on, with the sun bright in the sky. It reached the zenith.

Lunch followed, there at the corrals.

Bart ate with the others, then lay back in the shade to watch the clouds roll by.

Dick came over to sit beside him, and Helen and Tasy, who'd come up to eat with the men.

The bawling of the cattle went ceaselessly on, but Bart did not hear it. He could only rest and eat and finally walk over to examine Pirate's shoe.

"So far so good," he said to Danny who'd come along.

Then Frank rose to tighten the girth on his horse and remount. It was the signal for the afternoon branding to begin.

Bart forgot about Pirate's foot then. He forgot everything but the fact that he was part of the Kukaiau at branding time. He caught calf after calf. He raced with Danny.

They kept count.

Danny started it with "One!" as he dragged his calf by.

Bart grinned and took up the challenge. Just between them, for Frank would not have liked it, harmless as it was.

"One here," Bart said, and reached to catch a calf.

"Two!" Danny said, and dragged a second calf to the fire.

"Two here," Bart said, and caught his second.

They ran their string to five.

Then suddenly Danny said, "Six here——" and started for the fire, but his loop was empty.

Bart kept a straight face.

"Six here," he said, and dropped his loop over the nearest calf and moved toward the fire.

"Tomorrow," Danny promised.

And tomorrow it was the same. "One here," Danny said, and the contest went on.

"One here," Bart echoed. It seemed as though Pirate had entered into the fun. He moved with pride and precision and always with the minimum of effort.

"Two, three, four, five," the boys sang out. Then, suddenly, it was Bart's loop that was empty.

At last the final morning of the last day of branding arrived.

Bart and Danny rode their horses down to the gate. Off on the hills the branded calves and their mothers grazed. Five hundred head yet remained in the corrals to be done.

An ocean mist sifted up through the trees, through which the sun tried to break.

"We're even in the contest," Danny said, with a wide smile. "This is the day I'll beat you out."

"Maybe," Bart said. "Maybe not."

He let a hand slip down along Pirate's neck, then dismounted to clean out around the shoe.

The men came down to the fire and Dick and John and two other men to handle the irons.

Frank rode into the corral, followed by Kim, who would rope today, and Danny and Bart.

The work went on.

"Later, when we're nearing the end and get warmed up," Danny said, "we'll compete again."

Bart agreed.

They caught a calf each and moved for the fire.

"Just give me the high sign," Bart said. "Any time." He grinned and turned with his calf to the fire.

The work went on in earnest until well into the afternoon. Then, as Danny and Bart had moved to the fire with a calf and rode toward the herd, Danny turned in his saddle and asked, "How about now?"

"Fine," Bart said.

They reached the cows to press close.

The cows separated. A calf broke free. Danny dropped his rope and pulled.

"One here," he said, and dragged the bawling calf smartly toward the fire.

"One here," Bart sang out, and did the same.

"Two here," Danny said.

"Two here," Bart added.

So it went with neither boy missing a throw.

"Five, six, seven, eight, nine, ten," they counted.

Frank finally said, "All right, you two. I know what's been going on." But he didn't seem to mind.

The herd dwindled. There finally remained but four calves, and the score stood at fifteen each for the two boys.

Four days of grueling work had passed, one more than they'd figured. Now, with the end in sight, the men relaxed to enjoy this bit of fun.

"Sixteen," Danny sang out, and pulled his calf to the fire.

"Sixteen," Bart said and followed. His heart swelled with pride at the precision of Pirate beneath him.

"Seventeen," Danny said.

"Seventeen," Bart echoed.

"Eighteen," Danny's voice rang out. He smiled his old familiar smile and pulled his calf to the handlers.

"Eighteen," Bart said, and his own calf was in their hands.

"Nineteen."

"Nineteen."

But one calf remained, and it was Danny's throw. If he caught it he'd win.

"Twen—ty!" he said, but he gazed ruefully at his empty loop. His horse had turned too quickly and the throw had been short. The calf still stood beside its mother.

Bart's head did a quick bit of thinking. Danny had

done so much for him, should he miss too? But there was Pirate, moving toward the calf, and Dick watching, and anyway, you had to shoot square. He couldn't miss on purpose. He wouldn't. His loop licked down and there was the calf's leg.

Bart gave the rope a flip and silently moved to the fire. No use calling it out. Everybody knew it was the twentieth calf and that he'd won, and Pirate.

"There's still the cattle loading this fall," Danny said. "I'll get you then."

Bart grinned back at Danny. He felt wonderful. Pirate had gone through the cattle drive and the branding. It looked as though the shoe was going to hold.

"We'll see about that," he said.

The gate widened and the last cows and calves moved out across the meadow.

How it happened then, no one could ever tell.

A calf darted back into the corral.

"Let it go," Frank called sharply.

Bart nodded and pulled on the reins, but the big horse swung toward the calf. He reached him and turned again and hazed the fleeing calf toward the gate.

Bart, still green to the saddle under strain, felt his body slant to throw the big horse off balance. He was conscious of Pirate's fight to right himself and of his failure to make it.

A moment more and the stallion staggered, tried to catch himself, and finally sloughed off to one side and to the ground.

Bart shot over his head to roll harmlessly in the soft corral dirt and spring to his feet.

He knew even before he could reach the horse, who'd struggled to his feet and stood with his right forehoof dangling in the air, what had happened.

"He's overreached," Danny said, and slipped from his saddle to ease the horse's foot with his hands.

"Yes," Bart said dully. "He's overreached." He stared at the torn hoof and still couldn't believe that it had happened.

"Danny'll get the pincers to pull the shoes," Dick said gently.

Bart looked at Pirate's dangling foot. He was tempted to forget everything but this horse. But he looked at the cows on the hills and the men around him. There would be the beef shipping in the fall and the ceaseless work of the Kukaiau that must go on.

"Well, I'm not afoot," he said, and forced a smile. "There's always Ghost."

A murmur of admiration for him ran around the group.

"Yes," Dick added softly. He knew what Bart thought. That Pirate's and his battle was only part of the struggle —his own private one, really. "There's always Ghost."

Bart turned then to take the pincers from Danny and rip the shoes from Pirate's three good hoofs and the one that had torn still farther into the foot.

Chapter 15

TIME OUT

Hours later Bart came into his bedroom and slumped to a chair. For a moment he stared vacantly through the opened window toward the clump of houses down the road. Then he hauled out pen and paper and started a letter.

"Dear Doc: Well, I put a shoe on Pirate and it was a floperoo. He overreached when he moved after a calf and tore it off." Bart went on to describe the accident in detail. He told Doc about beating Danny in the roping and how the big horse had acted. "He's the greatest," he said. "The greatest—but the shoe didn't hold, and what am I going to do now?"

All at once, from down the road, came the voices of three boys. Bart glanced up and saw Keoki Hailaue, Kim's little boy, Lao, and Arthur Holi Mae.

"I'm Pirate," Lao declared. "My foot's hurt." He had a rag wrapped around it and danced in a circle in the dust. "The shoe's off and I'll never be any good again. Never."

"You will too," Arthur protested. "I'll take you to Bart. He'll fix you up, just like my dad says he's going to fix Pirate."

"I won't either. There's no place to nail the shoe."

"You will too. My dad says Bart's going to make a shoe for him that'll hold. You'll see."

Bart closed the letter with a rueful smile, then sealed it, and walked out of the room. He got a bucket and filled it with hot water, then moved out to the saddling shed.

Pirate stood there on three legs. The big horse nuzzled him as he came close and bit playfully at his arm.

"Hi, boy," Bart said, and sat down to put the foot in water.

The moon came up as he sat there and cast eerie shadows along the barn wall.

Suddenly he was surrounded by a group of ten and twelve-year-old boys and a few girls. They sat down in a circle around him.

A boy that looked like Keoki's older brother said, "Mrs. Hunter tells us you're going to teach us to play for the Christmas entertainment."

"Yes," another boy went on, "she says you're going to form a band," and brought out a harmonica.

As if by magic other harmonicas appeared.

Bart didn't see Dick and Homer step into the shed. They lingered back in the shadows. He couldn't see anything but this group of eager youngsters.

"She says you're going to really surprise us at Christmas too," another boy said. "That you're going to figure out a way for Santa Claus to come that we'll n—e—v—e—rr guess."

"Yes."

"That's right."

Bart sat back on his heels. The moonlight came in to search out each child's face. He could hear the horses in the paddock and the throb of life around him. It was a deep current that swept him along.

He reached into his own pocket, put his harmonica to his lips, and sounded a chord.

"Okay, kids," he said. "We'll start with 'Jingle Bells.' Anybody know 'Jingle Bells'?"

"No."

"But we know the 'Hawaiian Wedding Song'!" The voices were enthusiastic.

"Why don't we start with the 'Wedding Song'?" Bart suggested.

They all put harmonicas to their lips and the slow, beautiful wedding song of centuries swelled on the night air. They played "Hawaiian Wedding Song" through twice, then Bart taught them "Jingle Bells."

"Okay, now, it's time to go to bed," Bart said. "We'll have another session tomorrow night, and plenty of nights until we get good for Christmas. That's a promise."

"A week from tomorrow night, you mean," Dick said as he stepped closer. "Bart's going on a trip for me."

Bart stood up, then turned to Dick.

"No," he protested. "That is——" He put his hand on Pirate's neck.

Dick came close to Bart and put a hand on his shoulder.

"Sometimes when you've got a problem it pays to take time out, to stand off and take a look at it from a distance," he said.

Bart hesitated.

Dick's hand tightened.

"I've gotten word there are some frying-pan cattle down on the slopes of Mauna Loa. I want you and Danny to bring them home," he went on, then added with a smile, "There's to be a *luau* at Kailua beach. Helen and I'll be there. You can get some real Hawaiian food there, too, Bart."

"But what about Pirate?"

"I'll keep an eye on him while you're away. You'll come back rested and Pirate'll be waiting for you."

Bart nodded. He'd hear from Doc. It would be all right.

"Fine," he said, and lifted Pirate's foot out of the bucket to pour some oil over it.

Dick moved on to the house and the boys and girls disappeared.

Minutes later Bart and Homer walked out of the saddling shed, after turning Pirate loose in the paddock.

"I've got to roll," Homer said. "I'm going back to camp tonight and then on to Kailua area. See you there perhaps."

"Sure, perhaps." Bart nodded and paused to watch Homer ride up the trail, then walked to the house and his room.

"Time out, until I hear from Larry," he said, and rolled into bed.

Chapter 16

THE LAVA TUBE

Two mornings later Bart rode out on the little gray Ghost. Danny, on his black rode with him.

Pirate ran along the paddock fence and nickered and craned his neck as much as to say, "Why aren't you riding me?"

"Your turn will come at the cattle loading," Bart called. But Pirate still continued to nicker and limp along the fence line. Dick Hunter came from the house to put a hand on Bart's stirrup.

"I don't say there are any cattle there," he said. "But if there are, bring them in. And be careful, you're riding into lava-tube country."

Bart realized again how sensible Dick was. Lava country had killed Des, but Dick wasn't going to keep Bart wrapped in cotton wool.

"We'll do our best," Bart said.

"So long, then." Dick's hand tightened on Bart's knee, then dropped.

Bart pressed his heels to Ghost and rode south with

Danny. They rode through Tim Field, Dairy Field, then out into the Forest Reserve—that vast area of cinder cones, grass, and scrub trees.

"We should pick up Homer down at Kailua," Danny said. "He was supposed to go down there."

Bart nodded. "He said he'd be around that area."

They rode on toward the Saddle Back, an area that lay between the two high peaks of Mauna Kea and Mauna Loa. Before long they passed a herd of cattle and swung through them.

Bart looked sharply for brands, but there were no frying-pan cattle among them. Just the big P of the Parker ranch.

"You did that like a real cowman," Danny said.

Bart realized that it was true. It was becoming second nature for him now to look for stock, to size them up and estimate how much they'd weigh, and check for brands.

After another hour's ride they sighted a set of buildings off to the right.

"That's the Parker ranch," Danny said. "Second largest ranch in the whole United States."

Bart turned in his saddle to study the low buildings that sprawled across a wide flat field.

"Doc used to take care of their stock," he said. "He was there a great deal, riding their range."

"Then he must have ridden this land we're on right here," Danny said.

Bart reined up his horse and looked more closely

around him. At Mauna Kea that reared high in the
clouds, at the Saddle Back between, and Mauna Loa,
the volcanic mountain to the south. It made Doc seem
very close and brought the thought: I wish he were here
right now. He'd know what to do about Pirate's foot.

"Well, we'd better move along," Danny reminded
him. "We've got a lot of ground to cover before
night."

"Right," Bart said and rode on.

They pushed south at a trot, through wild gooseberry
and laurel and low shrubs, and kept a sharp lookout
for cattle that might be hidden in the brush. But though
they rode through several bunches of cattle, they found
none with the frying-pan brand.

At noon they stopped to eat, while their horses grazed.
Bart chose a shady bush under which to fling himself.
But suddenly, as he moved to go under it, the small
tree seemed to explode right before him. He heard a deep
grunt and jumped aside just in time to miss a huge
tusked wild boar.

Danny laughed as the tusker grunted away into the
trees.

"Pretty low altitude for that fellow," he said. "They
usually range higher in the mountain area." He grinned
at Bart. "Guess he wanted to give you a scare."

"Well, he certainly succeeded," Bart said with a grim-
ace. He chose another bush and sat down to eat his
lunch.

After an hour to rest their horses they pushed anxiously

on. It bothered them that they'd found no stock, for Dick Hunter wasn't given to sending out riders unless he was pretty sure there would be stock to bring in.

They rode on until they reached the Saddle Back. The afternoon sun waned and slipped into the sea. A soft night wind came up. Off toward the hills a bunch of nene geese flew across the sky line.

"Homer's pets," Danny said as he stared around at the landscape empty of cattle. "We'll have to tell him about them."

At dark they reached a small creek and drew rein.

"This is as good a place as any," Danny said, and slipped from his saddle. "We'll camp here tonight and really get going tomorrow."

Bart dismounted to unsaddle his gray and hobble him, then helped Danny build a fire of dead manzanita wood. In an hour they'd eaten and stretched out on their saddle blankets. Bart fished out his harmonica and lay flat on his back playing softly as the stars came out, letting the wonder of being a real cowboy like Danny here and Frank Correia amaze him.

After a while he stopped playing and turned to Danny.

"Do you think I'll ever ride Pirate out on a job like this?" he asked.

"Sure you will," Danny declared.

Bart smiled.

"You're as sure as John Holi Mae's Arthur," he said and told Danny about Lao's "sore foot" game.

"He's not the only one who's sure," Danny said,

solemn for once. "The men at the ranch are all betting you'll make it."

Bart shook his head.

"If I were only half as sure," he said.

Danny yawned and stretched.

"Well, morning comes early, and tomorrow we've really got to deliver." He rolled in his blanket, then grinned across at Bart. "Call me when breakfast's ready, my good man," he said.

Bart reached over to smother Danny's head in his blanket, then turned over to wrap himself in his own.

Daylight wakened them. They sat up, shivering with the early-morning cold, then rustled a fire and cooked bacon and made coffee.

"No cattle," Danny said as he stared around him. "There's always the chance that some might have grazed close during the night."

"Not a thing," Bart agreed, and stared off toward the sea that glistened under the morning sun.

In an hour they'd saddled and ridden on. They entered a closely populated area of tiny coffee plantations interspersed with open lands.

"This is lava-tube area," Danny said, "so watch it, Bart. There's always a chance that your horse will break through one of them."

"I will," Bart said, and tightened his hold on Ghost's reins.

They rode on, and up a slope, then paused to wind their horses.

Danny nodded to a little half-moon bay.

"Kailua," he said. "Where you came in on the plane. And that other bay to the south with the white monument on the water's edge is Kealakekua."

"Dick and I drove there one night." Bart smiled at the memory.

After a ride of perhaps twenty minutes they heard the low moo of cattle and swung to ride through them. But nothing with the frying-pan brand showed up.

At about ten o'clock they rounded a point and met four native boys and three girls. They came swinging down the trail from the slopes of Mauna Loa. Their arms were loaded with plants and some fruit. A big boy with black hair and sturdy brown body led them.

"That's Eddie Kaa," Danny said as they came up, then said, "Hi, Eddie." He turned to introduce Bart. "This is Bart Holiday, Eddie; he's come to stay at the Kukaiau."

"Yes, I know," Eddie said.

Bart was startled. News sure traveled far on this island —and fast!

"We're having a *luau* tonight," Eddie said. "We'd like to have both of you come, if you will.'

Danny thanked him.

"If we get through in time," he said. "If we do or we don't find any frying-pan cattle by night. You didn't see any up that way, did you?"

Eddie shook his head.

"Well, we'll see," Danny said. "Thanks for the invitation."

The group filed on, and Bart and Danny rode south. They forged ahead until the sun lay well toward the sea. They had spotted no cattle for an hour and rode glumly.

At length they drew rein just above a black reef that stretched out into the sea.

"The City of Refuge," Danny said, in answer to Bart's unspoken question. "In the olden days, during bloody tribal wars, anyone who reached here was assured of sanctuary." Danny grinned and went on, "If we don't find Dick Hunter's cattle we'd better head for there ourselves."

Bart smiled ruefully. Of course it was Danny's joke, but it brought sharply home how futile their trip had been so far.

"Well, we'd better get going," Danny said, and led the way. "Watch it, this whole slope is honeycombed with lava tubes."

Bart picked up his reins and followed Danny.

At length they reached the division fence and the end of the area they'd been told to cover. The two boys turned in their saddles to stare at one another.

"Well, we'll just have to move back on lower ground and hope," Danny said.

Bart agreed. The wind whistled lonesomely in the scrub bushes around them. Off toward the sea they could hear the montonous sound of the surf. Bart pushed his gray to ride on, when suddenly, almost before them, a muley steer poked his white-faced head through the brush.

Even at a distance Bart could read the brand, as the steer came on out.

"Well, welcome home," he said.

"You said it," Danny agreed. For behind this steer stood seven of his mates with the frying-pan iron spread along their ribs.

The boys moved forward.

Bart circled the herd at a gallop. Suddenly his horse seemed to hesitate, then dropped a foot into the ground and rolled to the grass.

Bart managed to stay in the saddle until the gallant little gray hit the ground, then stepped from the saddle.

Danny came riding up and wiped the sweat from his forehead, as Ghost struggled to his feet.

"Whew!" he exclaimed. "Lucky you weren't going any faster."

Bart turned to check Ghost's foot, which seemed all right, then swung back to Danny.

"Is that how Des was killed?" he asked.

Danny nodded and slipped from his horse to examine the hole, then dropped flat to the ground.

"It's a lava tube all right," he said. "And it looks like one that's never been explored. I can see the bottom right there." He sat up to stare at Bart. "This is Homer's line," he went on. "But maybe we can drop down into it and take a look around. It may be a burial tube where the early Hawaiian natives buried their dead to keep them from their enemies. If we find anything, we can tell Homer about it tonight at Kailua."

Bart agreed. It would be fun to explore the tube.

They tied their horses to a tree and made sure that the steers weren't drifting away, then came back to the tube.

"I'll take the lead," Danny said, then dropped through the hole.

Bart followed.

They found themselves about four feet underground in a tube that led off into the dark. Danny struck a match and they moved cautiously along to a small rounded area with a low benchlike seating around the edge.

Suddenly, as they stared around, a familiar voice hailed them from the entrance.

"Come out of there, I know you."

"Homer," Danny said. "That's great. Come on in, we've found something for you."

Homer dropped into the tube and came toward them by the flash of his powerful light.

"I was looking for you," he said, "and trailed you here."

They moved along through the room that proved empty.

"Maybe there'll be another," Homer said. "They usually buried their dead as far as possible from an entrance."

They walked and crawled through three more room-like areas and paused.

"No good," Danny said.

Bart thought they'd better get out and go on. It was time to get the cattle and head for the ranch.

"Just one more room," Homer said. "Of course I'll come back and explore it all, but right now——" He passed through a small opening that led to another room.

His sudden quiet seemed ominous. Then all at once Bart and Danny moved in beside Homer and they could see why he'd been so silent.

By the flashlight's glare they saw skeletons swathed in fabulous tapa cloth, which Bart knew was beaten inner bark of the *wauke* tree. War clubs with wooden handles and stone heads lay beside them on the bench shelf.

Bart picked up a shark-tooth dagger. It gave him a peculiar feeling along his midriff.

Homer reverently touched a ceremonial mantle. The flashlight showed it to be made of iridescent feathers.

"Robes of the kings," he said. "Doctor Bryan of the Bishop Museum will surely like to hear of this." He moved on to examine more skeletons and the utensils and war weapons lying beside them.

At length, as the boys became more restless, Homer turned to lead them out of the tube.

"Whew!" Danny said, and drew a deep breath as they climbed from the hole. "How about a dip in the ocean tonight?"

Bart grinned, after making sure that the cattle were close by.

"You said it," he exclaimed. "Come on."

They mounted and moved the steers north.

"We'll make it to Kailua," Danny said. "We can corral them there for the night and get an early start for home in the morning."

"Good, I'll ride with you," Homer said. "I'm going to the *luau* tonight."

The *luau*! Bart's and Danny's eyes met. They'd forgotten all about it, but why not, now that they had the cattle?

"So are we," Danny said, and flipped his rope at a steer's heels.

Chapter 17

THE LUAU

At nine o'clock that night Bart and Danny, with Homer trailing, hazed their eight steers down the main street of Kailua. As they reached a familiar corner they turned up a side street to a small corral.

A huge dark-skinned man in a colored shirt came out of his house and over to them.

Danny wiped his forehead with a grimy hand and gazed toward the beach. Through the trees glowed a campfire, and before it perhaps fifty Hawaiian boys and girls danced to the low music of ukuleles.

Homer said to the man, "These are friends of mine from the Kukaiau ranch."

"From the Kukaiau," the man repeated. "Then there will be hay and this corral for their stock for tonight."

"Good," Danny said. "Whew! I'm hungry."

Bart took off his hat and wiped his forehead. He wished they were home. What was Pirate doing? Had the inflammation in his foot subsided?

"Me too," he managed.

"Then what are we waiting for?"

"Daylight," Bart told himself. "So we can get on." But to Danny he said, "Nothing, let's go."

They corralled the steers, tended their saddle horses, and turned to go.

"You can sleep with me at the station," Homer said. "You go along to the *luau*. I've got to write a report on that cave to Doctor Bryan. I'll be along. If you should want to swim, go by the station. You know where it is, Danny."

"Do I?" Danny exclaimed. "Come on, Bart." He led the way toward the firelight. As Bart trailed along, he saw Eddie Kaa and four of the others he'd seen on the trail.

Edie Holi Mae waved to him from across a table set on the ground and loaded with gourds filled with lichens and shrimps from the sea. Beneath the gourds and earthenware bowls were spread wide green ti leaves.

Nearby three brown-skinned boys rolled heavy round stones.

"*Umaliakus*," Danny explained. "It's an old Hawaiian game."

Bart was looking for Dick Hunter, but he was not in sight.

A wonderful fragrance of cooked pork and yams filled the air.

"We've got just time for a swim," Danny said. "Let's go."

"After two long hot days in the saddle, that'll be

wonderful," Bart said, and made for the beach. They found Homer's cabin along the shore and dug up two pairs of trunks, to don them, then run for the water.

Danny reached the waves first and dived under a huge roller.

Bart slipped beneath it too, with a flat, skillful dive. They swam for a quarter of a mile out into the surf, then came back to the beach. They raced one another. They found a surfboard and Danny gave Bart a lesson in surf riding.

Suddenly a gong sounded from the direction of the fire and a song of feasting came out on the night air.

"It's time," Danny said. "And boy, am I ready!"

They raced in on a breaker, then to the cabin to dress.

"Dick's got to be here now," Bart told himself. But as they reached the firelight, to glance along the girls and boys seated at the table, he could see that neither Helen nor Dick was there.

Eddie opened the imu or barbecue pit, and the girls began to fill the gourds with roast pig and poi.

Bart found himself beside Edie Holi Mae, who'd come to sit on his left. He asked if she'd seen the Hunters.

"No, but they're coming," she said.

Then suddenly he did see them coming through the giant palms and across the grass. Tasy was with them, and Dick was laughing at something Helen had said.

They waved to him, and Dick held up his thumb and finger to make a circle.

Bart heaved a sigh of relief, and suddenly the wonderful odor of food was overpowering. He'd never been
so hungry in his life.

The music went on, the food came around, and the
soft wind sighed through the trees.

Down the beach under the moonlight the rollers came
in, their phosphorescence making them seem like lighted
waves.

Bart leaned forward and drank deeply from a gourd.

Tasy came to sit on his right, and Dick and Helen
across the table from him.

"Pirate's all right," Dick said.

"Good," Bart said, and picked up some roast pork in
his fingers and put it into his mouth. It was too soon to
hear from Doc, but when he did, Doc would tell him
what to do.

Bart ate until he couldn't hold another bite. Around
him, native boys and girls fished poi from the bowl
with brown fingers and licked them clean.

At length all the food was gone—the pork, the lichens
from the rocks, the shrimp from the sea.

Bart leaned back against a tall palm tree. Three Hawaiian boys grouped close by with their ukuleles and
began a soft Hawaiian melody.

Others rose to dance, and all at once there was Edie
right in front of Bart with outstretched hands.

"Me, hula?" Bart exclaimed, and made a motion of
sinking lower into the sand.

"Surely."

Dick grinned from across the table of ti leaves.

"If you're going to be a Hawaiian, Bart," he said.

If he were? Bart wondered. It was Helen's smile of encouragement that decided Bart. If she wanted him to learn Hawaiian ways, he darned well would.

"Okay," he said to Edie as he rose. "On one condition." He turned to watch the waves breaking far out, the white combers that raced like wild white horses for the shore. "That when we finish you'll come surfboarding in the moonlight."

"That won't be hard to take," Edie said, and led the way to the circle of dancers.

Edie showed him how to hold his hands; how to move his hips and feet to the rhythm of the music.

Bart moved across the grass, all arms and legs.

"Good! Good!" came soft cries around him.

"I'll bet." He laughed, but kept right on.

The music changed to a fast rhythm, and Bart found himself swept into it in spite of himself. They danced and danced, until the moon rose high in the sky, and everything seemed to take on a magical cloak of brilliant shimmering silver.

At length the beat of the waves on the shore could not be further ignored. Almost by mutual consent the music halted and Bart found himself the center of a group that ran toward the waves and into them.

Surfboards appeared as if by magic.

A dark lithe boy thrust one into Bart's hands and motioned to the waves that still broke far from shore.

Edie, beside him, clutched one.

"Come on," she said, above his protests that he wasn't too good. "I'll help you." She ran across the sand and into the sea.

They swam out and out and out, pushing their boards ahead of them. At length they paused for a moment.

Bart thought he'd never seen anything more beautiful. He caught the lines of little Hailua and, behind it, the swell of the land that swept to form a pass between Mauna Loa to the right and Mauna Kea to the left.

Edie had climbed to her board and paddled furiously toward shore.

"Quick, Bart, paddle, faster, faster, faster——"

Bart caught sight of a huge wave bearing down upon them as he, too, stretched on his board.

"Quick, paddle faster, faster, faster——," Edie called, paddling furiously as she lay on her surfboard.

Bart paddled faster and faster.

Suddenly the wave was upon them.

"Now!" Edie called, and climbed to her feet.

Bart followed her lead as best he could and rose erect.

Suddenly they were caught up by the wave. They raced toward shore, borne by the mighty wall of sparkling water.

"Whee!" Edie called.

"Whee——" Bart began, then tumbled headlong to be churned over and over.

"You'll learn." Edie laughed.

Bart's answer was to retrieve his board and head out to sea.

Hours later they swam toward shore and the dying campfire.

Dick and Helen had long since gone. The village lay sleeping under the waning moon.

Edie paused shyly beside the truck, loaded with other young people from up and down Kona coast.

"See you back at the ranch," she said softly.

Bart nodded as Danny came by.

"Yes, at the ranch," he said, "and thanks, Edie. It was wonderful. It was swell!"

He moved after Danny toward Homer's hut and bed.

Chapter 18

"COOL OFF!"

It took Bart and Danny four days to drive the steers from Kailua to the Kukaiau ranch buildings. They were fat and couldn't stand to be crowded.

At length, in the late afternoon of the fourth day, they pushed the cattle through the gate and into the corral beyond the barn.

Pirate came limping along the paddock fence, whinnying and nickering, as much as to say, "Well, it's about time." Bart saw that the horse was even more lame than before he'd ripped the shoe from his foot.

Bart's hand tightened on his reins, but he just pushed on toward the barn. Doc's letter wouldn't be along for a few days yet, but when it came he'd tell him what to do. He'd probably want new measurements for Bateman to try again.

But before he reached the saddling shed, Tasy ran out of the house and toward him.

"A letter from Doc Holiday," she said. "Air mail, special delivery."

Good old Doc, he was right on the ball. He did a rapid calculation as he took the letter from Tasy's hand and saw that it was postmarked Chicago. What was Doc doing there? This was the fastest letter he ever hoped to get, and the best.

Danny said, "I'll go on down to the barn and look after my horse."

"Sure, sure," Bart said. Without waiting to dismount, he flung his leg across the tree of his saddle and ripped the letter open.

"Dear Bart: I got your letter, and all I can say is, 'Take it easy.' Do you expect miracles? I'm not surprised that the shoe was a floperoo and that he tore it off. I'll have to let you have it straight. Are you sure Pirate's falling wasn't your fault? That you weren't out of balance in the saddle when he made that lunge and you threw him out too?"

Bart gulped and stopped reading, then went on, "How do you expect to do it all in a few short weeks, or months? Take it easy. And what of that little gray Ghost you're riding? What kind of a break are you giving him? If I was that horse I'd throw you so high the birds would build nests in your hair."

Bart stopped reading and looked down at the gallant little horse who'd carried him through the week; who stood now, sweaty and tired, without food or water while he read this letter.

"As far as the shoe goes, I showed it to Bateman and he's gone as far as he can. He says you're on your own now. But he also says you're pretty handy, and, if I remember, Dick's got a well-equipped shop—so—— Do your stuff, and if you get a shoe on Pirate that'll hold by next June you'll be lucky. And now let me tell you something, Bart." Here Doc would be mussing his hair with a freckled hand and his gray-green eyes would be screwed up. Bart could almost see him. "This is a problem, see? It's the first big one you've had, and how you handle it will probably be the way you handle problems the rest of your life." Bart paused as the drone of the Hilo-to-Honolulu plane going over reached him, then went on reading: "I'll get on a soapbox now, Bart. In this world you've got to have patience and think of others with their problems as you work out your own. Didn't I hear you say something about a Christmas entertainment and Santa Claus coming? If I know Helen Hunter, she'll expect you to deliver on this too. So go to it.

"Yes, I'm in Chicago. I'm on the first leg of a trip that will take me twenty-five thousand miles, maybe to Hawaii. So long. I've got to catch the train. Good luck, Bart! Doc."

Bart stuffed the letter carefully in his leather coat pocket and straightened in his saddle.

"Patience!" he said aloud, then looked guiltily around as though all the ranch had looked over his shoulder and read Doc's words.

He rode down to the water trough and jumped to the ground to unbridle Ghost.

The little horse drank thirstily.

"And I let you stand there while I leaned on Doc for the answer to Pirate," Bart said contritely. "I'm sorry, little guy."

He led Ghost to the barn and tended him, then walked out to where Pirate stood with his neck over the fence and picked up his foot. He dug around the frog with his knife, then dropped it to the ground. Suddenly he took a deep breath.

Danny came to stand beside him.

"What'd Doc say?" Danny asked. "Must have been something by the look on your face."

Bart put a steadying hand on Pirate's shoulder and looked around the ranch, lying calm and quiet in the cool of approaching night. He felt the underneath surge of life here and its everlasting drive ahead.

"Plenty is right, Danny," he said. "I can see now that, like Doc says, I'm in this for a long pull." His hand tightened and then ran up along Pirate's flaxen mane. "I can see now that I was slightly nuts. I came here a green kid and, overnight, expected to work a miracle. I expected to put a shoe on Pirate and ride him off into glory like they do in the movies."

"Which picture?" Danny grinned.

"Okay, okay," Bart said. "But what I mean is, I've been a Nervous Nellie trying to do in a month what will probably take a year to do."

Danny nodded, then added truthfully, "If ever?"

Bart's hand went to smooth Pirate's foretop.

"Skip that," he said. "I'm going to do it."

Danny, for once, didn't smile. "I'm with you, Bart," he said. "And it's true, you did rush things."

"You could have told me."

"I didn't know it myself," Danny admitted. "I guess I wanted Pirate back as badly as you did. Well, so long. See you in the morning." He walked toward his house down the road.

Bart, with a last pat along Pirate's neck, moved to the ranch house and inside.

Helen looked up from a letter, also from Doc, and smiled.

"Larry's going around the world," she said.

"I know," Bart said.

Dick came out of his office and spoke to Bart. "A letter from Larry?" His eyes studied Bart's face.

Bart silently handed the letter to Dick who read it clear through, then folded the sheet into a compact whole. For a full minute he didn't move, beyond raising his eyes to Bart's.

Bart met Dick's as best he could.

"You realized this?" he asked.

"Somewhat," Dick said gently, "though not as clearly as Doc puts it here."

"Why didn't you tell me?"

"It's best to learn as you go along, Bart," Dick said. "As I do, as everyone does, by making mistakes and then ―"

"Making more," Bart said.

Dick extended the letter to Bart. "No, by straightening out the ones you make and trying to keep from making the same ones over again. Life is trial and error, trial and error with here and there a win."

"Thanks, Dick," he said at last. "It's like I was telling Danny. I've been rushing things, but now I'm set for the long pull."

Dick said, "The shop's yours, Bart. And anything I can do to help——"

Bart nodded gratefully and turned toward his room.

"Supper's in half an hour," Helen said softly.

"Thanks, Helen," Bart said, then walked over to her. He looked around to see that Tasy wasn't near, then motioned Dick close.

"I'm going right ahead with this harmonica band," he said. "You can count on that. And as I read Doc's letter out there in the yard, the Hilo plane went over. It gave me an idea for Santa Claus's arrival. How do you like this?"

He bent close and whispered to them for perhaps five minutes.

Helen laughed.

Dick thumped his knee with his hand and said, "Great! We'll do it that way."

Bart felt better. He moved to his room. The long pull lay ahead, but that was the way it was to be, with no miracles.

But as Bart sat down on his bed, the idea for a Christmas Santa Claus still bothered him. He got up and slipped out of doors.

Wolf rose from his kennel and came over to him, to yawn and stretch, then give a deep "rrrrfff, rrrrrffff!" toward Mauna Kea's High Country, answering a faint, distinguishable cry of wild dogs coursing their prey.

Bart drew him close, feeling his thick brown-gray fur, then walked down toward the blacksmith shop and the shed behind it.

For half an hour he studied the road that led from the shed to the entertainment hall. He stepped off the distance and measured the width of the trail with his eye.

At length he seemed satisfied.

"It can be done," he decided and turned back to his room.

"See you," he said to Wolf at the door.

The dog wagged his tail and turned to his kennel as Bart stepped inside.

Back in his room, Bart tossed his coat on the bed, then walked over to let the little brown myna bird out of his cage.

"You may not know it, Pete," he said, "but I've got a date with the blacksmith shop, several dates, in fact to make a shoe for Pirate." He put the bird on his shoulder and stroked his brown feathers with a gentle finger. "And you've got a date with a Christmas party as a star performer."

"Pete, Pete, Pete?" the bird queried and perked his head to one side, then pecked at Bart's left ear.

"Yes, Pete," Bart said. "Now, let's get busy. I've

been neglecting you." He put the bird on the table before him and made a knocking sound with his knuckles on the hard wood surface. "Okay, now you do it," he said. "In your throat, see?"

Patiently he worked to make the bird imitate the knocking sound, until finally Pete understood, and the sound came out clear and very like it.

Next Bart turned on his radio to get Honolulu.

"Now, boy," he said, as he brought Pete over on his finger to listen into the speaker. "Imitate this announcer."

For an hour he worked with Pete. Finally he was rewarded with Pete's first attempt at getting the man's accent and words.

"Good, really good," Bart said. "That's enough for tonight, boy." He put the bird back in his cage and felt for the first time since Pirate's accident that things were coming along fine.

Chapter 19

THE LIFE OF A COWBOY

For weeks then, and long into the early fall, Bart took his place with the other cow hands on the Kukaiau. He rose at dawn and saddled up Ghost. He ate breakfast with Dick and Helen and took his orders from Frank Correia like Danny and John Holi Mae, Kim, and all the other twenty-odd cowboys.

Through the hot humid Kona weather that blew from the southwest, and the trade winds that swooped down from the north, he worked with the cattle during the day, then at night moved down to the shop to light a fire in the forge, then sink a shoe deep in the coals and turn the blower with slow even strokes of the handle.

He made one shoe and tried it with Pirate's teeth nibbling playfully at his elbow and Pete perched on his back whistling and saying, "Hello, hello—this is John. This is John."

"John who?" Danny would come in to ask.

"John who, John who," Pete replied.

"Teach him something new," Bart suggested. "Teach him to smile like you."

"That doesn't make a noise," Danny said.

"Well, it almost does." Bart grinned and then grew serious as he dropped Pirate's foot to bury the shoe in the fire once more. "Pirate, Pirate," he said. "Will I ever make a shoe to handle that foot?"

So the work of the ranch went on, as well as his practice with the harmonica band and the top-secret task of bringing Santa Claus to the Kukaiau.

For it became known right after Bart's talk with Helen and Dick that something was happening in the room back of the blacksmith shop.

A lumber truck rolled up one night from Kukaiau. The next night a truck from Hilo brought some mysterious parts in a crate.

"Shoo!" Bart said, and scattered the boys and girls. They all ran down the road. It all became a secret with pounding and work in the back room.

"Of course, you're not to look," Bart said. "If you do that fellow in the beard may not show up at all."

"Of course not," they chorused.

"Scout's honor," Bart said.

"Scout's honor," they agreed.

Then all at once it was October 4th and time to round up the beef for the drive to Kawaihae and the loading on the big barge, *Homuula*, for Honolulu.

Bart moved out to the shop this last night with Pete perched on his shoulder. He leaned against the shop door and stared at Pirate who grazed in his paddock close by.

"Three months," he said. "And still I haven't gotten

a shoe that looks anything like a fit for him." He wiped his hand along his forehead. "I guess even you, Doc," he said to himself, "wouldn't think I was rushing things."

"Patience," a voice said.

Bart jumped and looked around, then realized that the voice came from his shoulder.

"Well"—he smiled—"where did you learn that?"

"Hello, John. Hello, John. Danny, Danny, Danny," Pete said, then made a knocking in his throat exactly like the knock on a door.

Bart stroked the feathers of the little brown bird with the yellow beak.

"Come in, come in," he said, then walked over to the forge. The fire from last night's work had died out, except for a few glowing coals. The shoe he'd fashioned, then dropped in disgust, lay across the anvil where he'd quitted it. It was a failure and he knew it. The weld hadn't taken properly. It was a rough job. "And brother, am I tired," he said. "And with the cattle drive coming up tomorrow." He took a step toward the house.

"Patience," Pete shrilled.

Bart lifted the bird down.

"You win," he said wryly.

Bart moved back to blow up the smoldering fire, then plunge a new shoe into the blaze. "Well, here goes," he said. But it was the same old story. The shoe wouldn't come right.

The next morning Bart walked down to slip a rope on Ghost and lead him to the saddling shed.

"Well, here she goes," Danny said beside him.

Pirate as usual followed, limping along.

Bart forced a grin. He'd worked faithfully, was saddle-hard, but this cattle loading was something else again. To rope the steers and drag them across the beach, then out to the boat, was hard and dangerous.

Bart put a rope on Pirate and tied him up beside Ghost. It made the big horse seem to belong.

The other riders didn't let on. They saddled in silence, though Bart realized that each would have given a month's pay to see Pirate ready to go.

He saddled Ghost and went to the house for breakfast.

In an hour everyone bridled his horse, mounted, and started quietly up the trail to round up the beef for the drive to Kawaihae.

Bart glanced back and flung up an arm to Pirate who ran along the fence.

"The long pull," he told himself, and settled deeper into his saddle. "Get on the ball, Holiday, and learn to balance yourself, so the next time Pirate makes a move you'll be right."

He leaned down to run a hand along Ghost's neck.

"All right, Ghost horse," he said. "Let's go."

The men then filed out across the paddock. Quietly, with but little shouting, just the press of being at the right place at the right time, they moved the cattle down the mountainside and out to the Forest Reserve.

"Drive them slow," Frank had said. "We don't want to run the fat off them if we can help it."

They trailed the long line of five hundred beef slowly through the trees, then out across the open grass area of the Parker ranch.

In the distance gleamed the sea, calm and smooth. At anchor rode the cattle boat, *Homuula*, as she waited for her cargo.

For two days they trailed the herd by day and bedded down at night, taking turns at night herding. Then on the evening of the third day they reached the sea.

Bart rode with Danny around the tired cattle and held them in a bunch. They'd graze them tonight, then in the morning corral them in small corrals and rope each steer to drag him out to a small waiting boat.

This boat in turn would tow the swimming cattle to the side of the *Homuula* where a big sling derrick would hoist them aboard.

"Our job's to get them to the rowboat," Danny said as they rode herd in the darkness that closed about them.

The Hilo plane bound for Honolulu droned over. Far to the east, Mauna Kea thrust her snow-covered tip into the clouds. While to the south, her uneasy sister, Mauna Loa, smouldered under constant volcanic pressure within.

The night herding went on.

Then Frank Correia and Kim rode out to relieve Bart and Danny, and they high-tailed it for their sleeping bags, to wait for dawn.

Bart tossed in his sleep and dreamed he was shoeing

Pirate. The shoe was not right, and Pirate kept nibbling the cork ends with his teeth. Suddenly his foot came off and lay there a few inches from Pirate.

Bart wakened in a sweat.

"Whew!"

"What's the matter?" Danny whispered.

"Nothing." Bart rolled over. He was glad to waken as he stared at the first light of dawn that streaked the eastern sky.

"Well, you were certainly making plenty of noise for nothing!" Danny teased.

Bart said, "Sorry," then rolled over and shut his eyes. But just then Frank rode into camp and said quietly, "It's that time, boys."

Bart rose with the rest and ate under the lightening sky.

In an hour the corralling began—the slow moving of cattle into a big corral, then into smaller ones, from which the men would rope the steers and drag them across the beach to the sea.

"Well, here goes," Danny sang out.

Bart tried to smile as he took down his rope. He realized as he studied a big red polled stear with a drooping ear that he faced his first test as a real cowboy on the Kukaiau. The roundup and the cattle drive had been one thing. But to rope one of these steers and drag him across the sand and out to the waiting boat was something else again.

"Pick a small steer, Bart," Danny said with a wide

grin. "Or he'll drag you to the boat and ship you and Ghost to Honolulu instead."

Bart tried to grin back. He made a loop and, avoiding the big lop-eared steer, roped a smaller one, then took his dallies and nodded to the gateman.

The steer came out of the corral and straight for the beach, bellowing and struggling against the rope.

Bart urged the gray to follow. They reached the water and suddenly the steer could see what would happen to him. With a low bellow of panic he turned and ran the length of the rope toward the shore.

Bart swung Ghost to face the fleeing brute. He braced himself against the shock as the slack left the rope and twelve hundred pounds of beef all but lifted Ghost from his feet.

At first Bart thought the horse would steady. But a second lunge tipped him to the sand. The rope ran off the saddle horn and the steer ran bellowing down the beach, tail in the air.

Frank rode down to Bart as he and Ghost struggled to their feet.

"I'll take him," Frank offered, but then he stopped and said, "Forget I said it." For Bart's face had the same look it had worn that day they'd been learning to rope in the open at the ranch.

Bart looked at the brute who'd stopped on the sand. He was big, but not as big as that other one in the corral that might be still to come.

"No," he said softly. "I'll handle him, Frank." He tested

his girth and climbed back into the saddle. That other steer, and more like him, were larger. Someone had to take them to the boat that lay offshore. He rode down the sand.

The steer threw up his head, then started to run.

Bart rode after him and caught the dangling rope, then made his dallies and again turned for the boat.

Again the steer tried to throw them. But this time, though Ghost all but left the sand, he did not go over.

"Good boy," Bart whispered. "Now!" He dragged the steer slowly up the beach to the water's edge, then out into the surf.

The horse swam easily, and though the steer threshed and bellowed, the wiry Ghost dragged him along. At length they were both swimming. Bart urged his horse alongside the boat. He turned his rope over to a boatman who ran another rope around the steer's horns and tied it to a crossbar, then handed Bart his own rope.

As Bart swam back for another steer, he knew that his hardest test lay ahead. For until he could quit picking them and take what came up, even to a steer as big as the lop-eared one, he'd not really have passed his test.

No one had said anything. No one would ever say anything. But it was there, and he had it to do. He roped a second steer of about the size of the first and after a struggle swam him to the boat.

Frank rode by.

"We're coming fine," he suggested. "How about laying off for a while?"

Bart shook his head.

"Have it your own way," Frank shrugged.

Bart leaned low in his saddle to whisper to the little gray horse. "This is it, Ghost," he said as they moved into the corral. He dropped his rope over the lop-eared steer, then signaled the gateman to open up.

The steer came out of the corral with a mighty bound, then ran wildly toward the open beach.

What followed then was talked of secretly on the ranch for years to come.

No one made a move to help. Dick went matter-of-factly on with his tallying. Danny, down the beach from Bart, pulled another steer toward the water. Frank purposely caught a big brute that would keep him plenty busy.

At the shore line Bart's ugly brute veered inland.

Bart reined Ghost to face the steer, then waited for the shock.

The rope tautened.

Ghost left the ground. The saddle creaked. But suddenly the horse regained the ground, then pushed backward to keep the rope taut.

The steer took another tack.

Again came that jolt as the rope tautened.

Five times the steer rushed. Five times horse and rider swerved to face the shock. Then all at once the steer tired, and slowly, quietly, doggedly the sweaty little horse, with Bart atop his back, dragged the hulking steer out into the water, first to wade, then to swim.

In minutes it was over.

The brute was lashed to the boat and Bart swam for shore.

Not a word was said. Business went on as usual. But Bart saw Dick hold up his hand to make an O with thumb and finger, as Frank smiled and nodded.

Bart knew then that he'd passed a big test as a cow hand on the Kukaiau.

Chapter 20

THERE AIN'T NO SANTA CLAUS

Late the following night Bart rode with Danny into the
Kukaiau yard. The main group of riders would reach the
ranch about eight o'clock.

"Guess, in our hurry, we sort of rode away from the
bunch," Danny said.

Bart dismounted and went to run a hand along Pirate's
neck.

"Guess so," he said, and looked down at the hoof.

"One thing is sure," Danny said. "If Pirate ever makes
the grade it'll be because of you and that anvil and those
twenty-odd shoes you've worked on."

Bart started to shake his head.

But the voices of Lao the believer and Keoki the
skeptic came from down the road.

"There is too a Santa Claus," came Lao's outraged
voice.

"Naw, there ain't neither. It's your pop dressed in
something an' pretending."

"It ain't."

"It is."

"It ain't. There'll always be a Santa Claus on the Kukaiau. Bart says so. He's going to bring him this year. He's promised."

Bart's hand tightened on Pirate's mane. "There'll be Santa Claus for you, too, Pirate, once Christmas is over," he said. "Sometime between then and the cattle drive I'll give you a shoe that'll do the trick."

"But right now," Danny reminded, "we've got to make Christmas come to the Kukaiau."

"Right," Bart agreed.

They moved down to the watering trough, then on to the saddling shed.

"Tonight?" Danny asked.

"Tonight," Bart agreed, and they ate supper, then went out to the shop to work on the secret of Santa Claus.

It seemed but a day but was almost two months later that Danny asked again, "Tonight?" and Bart nodded agreement.

It was Christmas Eve, and the two boys stood back of the blacksmith shop. Across the way the hall glowed with lights, and from the inside came the excited voices of the children of the Kukaiau.

"And there is a Santa Claus," Danny announced.

"Sure there is, and we've got to get going," Bart said.

They glanced up as Helen came from the house and toward them. Her arms were full of packages. She reached the boys and they took the parcels from her.

"Is everything ready?" she asked.

Bart looked inside the shop, then at Danny.

"As ready as human hands can make it," he said.

"Then we'll go down to the hall," Helen said. "And, Bart, after the program don't forget the waffles. Everything's ready on the kitchen table."

Bart wished fervently that Doc hadn't been so free with compliments on his cooking. And thinking of Doc reminded him of the letter saying he would be in Hong Kong today.

A hush came over the crowd as Helen, followed by Bart and Danny, entered.

Bart waved to Edie. Tasy was behind a huge pine tree that reached the ceiling.

In the front row sat Lao, his eyes wide with excitement, and beside him, Keoki, his face set with suspicious wisdom. Members of the harmonica band were easily identified by their excited faces.

Behind the children sat the men of the ranch with their families.

"If Doc were only here," Bart said softly to Helen.

Then suddenly the lights went down, except those on stage, and Dick appeared to start the program.

Tasy walked over to sit at the piano.

Whispers went around among the children.

"When's Santa coming? This ol' program. Wonder how he'll make it? Maybe he'll never find his way up here in the woods."

Tasy played the national anthem and everybody sang.

Then followed "Oh Susanna," "My Old Kentucky Home," and "Pack Up Your Troubles."

"Pack up your troubles," Bart whispered. "What troubles?" Brother, just let him at the shop and Pirate's foot when this was over and there wouldn't be any.

Tasy sang a song. Edie did a hula, her slender body swaying to the Hawaiian music of Kim's ukulele. Then Bart heard Dick's voice say, "And now, Bart Holiday and his harmonica band."

Bart waited for the boys and girls to file up as they'd rehearsed doing for weeks. When he saw that they were all in line, he walked to the stage. He raised his hand and put his own harmonica to his lips. Then came the soft music of ten harmonicas.

They played the "Wedding Song," "Aloha," and "Sweet Leilani," then followed with "I'm An Old Cow Hand," Kim imitating an old puncher with bowlegs.

Then suddenly it was over with a loud wave of applause. The band had to play an encore.

Danny did some card tricks, and Pete, perched on Bart's hand, imitated a radio announcer at Honolulu, then the knocking of a man on the door.

It was so real that little Lao almost started a riot by turning in his seat and saying in a high shrill voice, "There he is. There's Santa Claus at the door."

Then suddenly the lights went up and the program was over.

Danny and Bart raced out of the rear door and across the road to the shed.

In the hall Dick said, "Now we'll turn out the lights and put on the one down the road so we can see Santa Claus coming. But don't move from your seats or he night not come at all."

"Boy!" came Lao's voice. He shivered with excitement.

"Humph!" Keoki said. But he was careful not to stir from the hard pine bench on which he sat.

Then all at once came a roar from the road, a roar and a burst of headlight that flooded the roadway.

A stir ran through the audience. It was as though they'd been swept by a strong wind.

The noise increased.

"Sounds like an airplane," a boy called.

"Yea, a twin-engine job."

They rose.

The noise increased. It seemed to be coming from down the road that led to Kukaiau.

Then, at the roar of the motor without and the glow of the headlights that shone through the darkened hall windows, nothing would stop them. The crowd all surged forward and peered from the windows, then streamed out to the porch.

"It is a plane. She's landed. She's coming this way."

"Right up to the door," Lao's voice said triumphantly. His eyes went over the big homemade plane with the revolving propeller from a wrecking shop in Hilo and stopped on the sign: SANTA CLAUS SPECIAL. RIGHT FROM THE NORTH POLE, in big white letters.

"What'd I tell you? What'd I tell you?" he yelled at

Keoki who stood openmouthed, spellbound. They surged forward, then to one side as a big red figure leaped from the plane, struggled with a pack that stuck for a moment in the door, then disappeared inside the hall.

There never had been anything like it on the Kukaiau. All agreed as Santa Claus distributed the gifts. Santa Claus coming right up the road in a plane and where he landed no one knew. But he was here.

"I saw him land," Keoki declared. "Sure, right up there beyond the corrals. There's a big open place there."

Then suddenly the gifts were over and Santa Claus bolted for the door.

"So long, kids," he said in a voice cracked with the cold. "So long, see you next year."

He moved into the plane and turned it around.

"Now don't stir, kids. Don't look, or Santa Claus may not come back next year at all."

Not a child moved to watch the plane as it taxied down the road. The lights went out, and Santa had come again to the Kukaiau.

Later, in the big Hunter kitchen, Lao came up to Bart who was standing over the waffle iron.

"I said you'd make Santa Claus come, and you did," he said. "I guess you fooled Keoki."

Bart flipped a waffle onto Lao's plate. At least the waffles had turned out all right.

"Santa Claus always comes," he said.

Lao nodded and yawned, then went home with his mother.

"Remember that, Holiday," Bart whispered to himself. He glanced out of the window to Pirate's paddock. The big stallion's foot was ready to take a shoe. To wear in the paddock for two months, then be tested.

"Santa Claus always comes to the Kukaiau," he said, and helped himself to a waffle.

Chapter 21

THE FINAL SHOE

On the day after New Year's Bart led the limping Pirate into the blacksmith shop and tied him to the rail. Then he walked over to poke at the dead ashes in the forge. He whittled some shavings and struck a match, then lightly turned the bellows handle with his hand. When the shavings started to glow, he piled on coal slowly, to build a tiny mound of black dust.

Danny came in to take the handle.

"I'll manage the bellows," he said.

Bart walked over to the shoes along the wall and his eyes went down the row. He reached out to run a hand along the useless shoes. They were almost a complete record of his progress and failure thus far. This one he'd gotten too hot and burned the iron. This one was rough, and this one, the holes had been wrong.

He picked up the last shoe he'd done shortly before Christmas and walked over to lift Pirate's foot. He fitted it to the stallion's hoof as the big horse blew out his breath and sniffed along Bart's hair. It was old stuff now. Countless times he'd had him in here trying shoes on him.

Bart looked at the shoe and the hole along Pirate's foot, then flung the shoe to the floor. Would he ever make a shoe to cover that hole? One that would keep out the gravel and protect that injured frog from the cindered ground? He kicked the shoe to a pile of old iron and raised his eyes to meet Danny's.

"We'll start all over?" Danny asked.

"Yes, from scratch." Bart remembered the first time he'd shod Pirate. How confident he'd been then, and how unsure he felt now. "We'll start with the good feet," he said, and picked up the hoof trimmers.

Hours later, with his clothes clinging to him and moisture dripping off his nose, Bart dropped the last of Pirate's three good feet to the floor.

"Nice work," Danny said. "Tomorrow you can finish up."

Bart stared out of the door. Long shadows stood beneath the trees, and the wind had a hint of night in it. He walked over to take a deep drink of cool water from the jug, then came back to the anvil.

"Oh no," he said doggedly. "Right now." He stared at Danny, then at Pirate. "I've been sweating this thing out for weeks. It's now or never. You can go if you want to." He grasped the blower handle.

"My job," Danny said, and took it from his hand. "You can't fire me now."

Bart took down a new shoe from the rack. It was of finest blue steel and a six-ounce shoe, made by the Phoenix Horseshoe Manufacturing Company of Joliet, Illinois. He shoved it deep into the fire.

"A full two sizes smaller than his other shoes," Danny said.

"So what?" Bart replied. "If it fits."

Danny began to turn the bellows.

Bart forgot everything then but this bit of steel. He brought it out and shaped it, using all the skill he'd acquired from Bateman and his work here with Pirate. He put it on the stallion's foot and peered at it through the fumes that rose from the burning hoof. He tried it again and again and again.

Darkness came. He hardly knew when Danny snapped on the lights. Dick came in and without speaking went to bring him his supper on a tray.

Between fittings Bart ate two thick beef sandwiches and drank two cokes, then went on with his work.

He cut out a piece of flat steel and held it up beside the shoe.

"I'm going to build it up here," he explained. "Make a piece that will be like Pirate's missing hoof." His bloodshot eyes met Dick's in question.

Dick bent over it, as Bart put the cold shoe and the bit of steel together, then said, "It may work, if—if you can weld it to stay?"

Bart hadn't been working on this forge for months not to know.

"I can," he said, and buried the shoe and the steel in the fire. When they were hot, he put them together on the anvil. He threw on alum to bind them, then cunningly fitted them together with blows of his hammer.

Danny whistled in surprise and appreciation as he watched Bart fashion the shoe and weld the steel to it.

"Hey," he said. "Where'd you learn that?"

"Bateman," Bart said, and went on hammering.

In another hour he put the shoe down. It was done. He dropped it into the tempering water and walked to the door.

Night had fallen. A silver cheese bite of moon hung over the trees and a small wind rustled along the ground.

Wolf came to whine and poke his cold nose in Bart's palm, then move on to his kennel. An owl burst in full flight from an ohia and up along the Corn Field paddock.

Bart took a deep breath and turned around. "Now, boy," he said, and his heart hammered along his ribs in spite of himself. "We'll nail the shoe on and see if it takes the limp away."

He worked quickly then to nail the shoe and clinch it, then backed away. He untied Pirate's rope with trembling hands and led him out the door and along the rocky road, and Pirate didn't limp.

For a full minute Bart leaned against the horse, unable to believe it. He led him further and with the same result.

Danny took the rope and Bart dropped back to watch. Then he knew it was really true.

"He's okay," Danny said. "We'll try him on the cinders."

Bart exulted. "Yes."

But Doc's words, "What are you trying to do, work miracles?" came to him.

Bart swallowed. He'd almost been sucked into that trap. A year ago he would have. Now he shook his head and said, "We'll have to turn him loose for a month to get used to the shoes. Then we'll ride him and see."

Danny shook his head and murmured, "A month is a long time."

Bart wordlessly stripped Pirate's halter from his head and gave the stallion a light tap along his shoulder.

"Yes," he said. "It is." But he drew in his breath with pleasure as he watched the big horse sift up through the trees at a swinging, limp-free gallop.

A month later Bart stood in the paddock, bridle in hand, and watched the big horse come down through these same trees to him.

The sun shone; everything was wonderful. He slipped the bridle on and led Pirate to the barn for a saddle. He felt sure now that Pirate was fine. But he'd ride him today, up along the trail, then through the cinders. Slowly at first, then picking up speed as they rode.

Danny mounted his black.

Bart got on Pirate and they rode up along the trail, then out across the cinders. At the end of a mile Bart's eyes met Danny's in triumph.

"Fine," he exclaimed, then swung Pirate as though to turn a calf.

There was a slight clink.

Bart gulped and tried again.

Again it came, "Clink!"

Bart dropped to the ground and lifted Pirate's foot, then studied the shoe with anxious eyes.

"There it is," he said. "He's overreached again."

Bart dropped the foot and straightened. His throat was cotton-dry. He tried to swallow, and his eyes looked off across the trees. The wind sighed lonesomely around him and the hush of the mountains closed him in.

But suddenly his spine stiffened. He swung to Pirate and picked up the reins, then mounted. "It's back to the shop for you," he said, and rode down the hill and into the little red-painted building.

He ripped off the shoe and slumped to the forge. How long he sat there, Bart never knew.

Danny said, "I'll be back in a minute," and went out.

Keoki poked his head in, and Lao, and knew that they were not wanted.

Still Bart sat on. At length he slid to the floor and sat there with his back to the anvil. He tossed the shoe into the tub, half asleep. It made a slap and Bart roused to see Pirate drop his nose to sniff around his injured foot. Suddenly Bart's mind went back to that dream he'd had at Kawaihae, when Pirate's foot had seemed to be off the horse and the stallion had put his nose down to bite the ends of the shoe. As though he'd wanted to get rid of them.

Bart sat up to fish the shoe from the tub and suddenly his pulse leaped.

"Well, why don't we get rid of those points that hit when Pirate overreaches?" he said, and leaped toward the forge. "Have a round plate that covers the whole bottom of his foot?"

Two hours and three shoes later, Bart dropped Pirate's foot shod with a round shoe, a plate with no ends. He led the horse again to the paddock.

"Aren't you going to try him now?" Danny asked.

Bart shook his head. The temptation was strong.

"In April," he said shortly. "A week before the cattle drive. If that's a success, then the cattle drive itself and the branding will tell whether Pirate'll be a cow horse the rest of his life or—a hopeless derelict."

Chapter 22

SHOWDOWN

Three months later Bart walked out to saddle Pirate for the cattle drive. A strong Kona wind lashed the ohia trees and made little eddies of dust along the ground.

Danny passed and, said "Well, this is it," and couldn't muster his usual smile.

Bart tossed the saddle on and brought up the cinch, and he'd have given almost anything to have today and the branding days to follow over with.

"Yes," he said. "This is the showdown."

The men around Bart saddled with their usual jests but their talk seemed forced. They had all watched the test of Pirate's shoe the week before, which had gone off very well. But they knew that the real test lay ahead.

Dick came out of the house with Helen and Tasy, all talking of the cryptic letter from Doc and wondering when, if ever, he'd come. "Look for me when you see me," it had said, and that was all. But it was sent from Hong Kong from where a plane to Honolulu would only take days, then another to Kailua would be a matter of hours.

The men finished saddling and prepared to mount. The women came to decorate their hats with *leis*, but there was restraint in the air.

Bart picked up Pirate's foot with the round plate.

"No nicks along the base," he said. "No gravel under the shoe." He dropped the foot to the ground.

"That helps," Danny said, and mounted his black.

Bart agreed and also mounted, impatient to go.

Frank led the men up through the wind-whipped trees toward the summit to begin the cattle drive. At the top he glanced at the rocky ground beyond the trail.

"Bart," he said, "why don't you and Danny take the smooth, easy way back?"

Bart looked over at Dick and shook his head.

"The time's past for coddling Pirate," he said. "Now, let's see——"

"Let him ride with me," Dick said, and led the way out to where the cindered grass was filled with pumice hummocks.

The drive down the mountain began.

Anxious as he was, Bart could not help thrilling at the sight of cattle trailing down the slopes in an ever widening stream of bawling cows and calves.

At length they reached the gate and the cowboys began to silently push the cattle into the corral.

Bart worked with the rest and Pirate worked with him. The big horse pressed in close and his eyes flashed with pleasure at being in the thick of it.

Then the last cow and calf went into the corral and the gate clanked shut.

Bart dismounted as a bit of smoke from the branding fire came sifting over to him. It brought back sharply the branding time of last year and Pirate's torn shoe.

Dick rode over to dismount and lift the foot to examine it. There was a moment of quiet, like a held breath.

"Fine," he said at length, "fine," and dropped the hoof.

A murmur of pleasure ran around the group of men as Danny's laugh rang out.

Helen and Tasy moved down the hill toward the house, for it was late afternoon and not much branding would be done today.

"If Doc comes, I'll bring him up," Helen called to Dick.

Dick smiled and moved toward the corral. "If Doc comes," Dick answered, "he'll probably bring himself up."

Helen laughed and walked on.

Frank came riding over to Bart.

"There's enough ropers," he said. "You could take it easy this afternoon with Pirate; pick it up tomorrow."

"Or use Ghost," Dick said.

Bart looked off across the hills. "And let Doc come and find me dodging?" He picked up Pirate's reins and remounted. "Not a chance."

Frank's approving smile was very much the same as it had been down in the paddock the day he'd worked with Bart on roping. "Sure, Bart," he said, "I know what you mean," and nodded to the men.

The gate flung wide to let them in and the branding began.

The afternoon passed, and the next day, and the next.

Bart worked with the others and caught calf for calf and dragged them to the branding fire. The big horse beneath him worked smoothly, easily, and gracefully, and Bart forgot all about the foot.

At length he and Danny resumed their game.

"One," sang out Danny.

"One here," Bart echoed.

The day wore on, and at evening, with the branding-fire smoke hovering in the hills, there remained but few calves to be done.

"One," Danny said.

"One here," Bart said. He was so intent he didn't see a car drive up and a tall man with graying red hair and sharp blue eyes behind steel-rimmed spectacles leap out. He didn't see Dick go over and wring his hand, then turn to wave at the corral and the other man turn and look.

"Two," Danny went on.

"Two here," Bart added.

So the game went on, with, "Three, four, five, six, seven. . . ."

The men took it up and little bets were made: a bottle of pop against a ticket to the movies; a new rope against a pair of spurs. Suddenly the last calf was there beside its mother.

"Ten," Danny sang out, and his rope caught the calf. But the imp kicked free and ran back to its cow.

Bart swung Pirate close. He could feel the power and beauty of the big horse as he dropped his loop.

, "Ten," he said, and knew that he'd caught the calf, as Pirate automatically swerved for the fire.

But Bart's pleasure was short-lived. For now the calves and cows would be let out the gate. This was the danger moment as it had been last year.

His hands tightened on Pirate's reins.

"Bart!" Dick called to decoy him away. "Look who's here."

"Go on, Bart," Danny said under his breath. "No use pressing your luck."

Bart stubbornly shook his head. No use wrapping Pirate in cotton wool the rest of his life.

"Open the gate," he said. "Open her up."

The gate swung wide and the cattle moved out. Of course it happened as it always does when cattle are pushed through a gate. A calf ran back.

Bart waited for it. He'd known all along that it would happen. He really wanted it to happen. Now he drew in his breath and tightened his hands on his reins. All the months of work and his time at the anvil would make or break the golden palomino right here.

"Now, Pirate," he said, and gave the great horse his head.

For one long second there was a pause, then the big horse swung for the calf.

Bart, saddle-hard and skilled from months in the

work of the Kukaiau, rode as part of him. This time he didn't throw Pirate off balance.

In half a dozen mighty bounds the palomino circled the calf and pushed him out the gate.

Bart knew before the horse quit moving that he was all right, that he'd passed the test. He sat there numbly as Doc and Dick came toward him, and the corral dust drifted off around the grazing cattle, and knew that he'd won. He'd finally gotten a shoe on Pirate that would hold.

"Okay?" Danny asked.

"Okay," Bart said, and turned toward Doc. It was as simple as that and as sweet as life itself.

Then Doc and Dick reached his side.

Bart dismounted and Doc took his hand, then ran his other hand up to feel Bart's muscle.

"Hard," he said, and turned to smile quizzically at Dick. "Is he a good cowboy?"

"He's coming along," Dick said softly.

Doc swung to lift Pirate's foot and soberly examined it, then dropped it to the ground.

"Wonderful job, Bart," he said. "Wonderful."

For several minutes the two stood there with the sound of the cows bellowing for their calves drifting back in the evening hush. Dick and the punchers had gone, and nothing remained but the opened corral gate, the smell of cattle dust, and the rustle of the trees.

Doc was more thoughtful than usual, as though he had something on his mind.

They went down to the barn, Bart on Pirate and Doc

in his car, and Bart proudly showed him his locker, then unsaddled.

Doc, waiting for Bart to say something about going back to Nebraska, again lifted Pirate's foot and whistled and said, "I could do no better—not so well, in fact."

Bart pushed the horse out of the door. Pirate ran swiftly along the grass, then dropped his head to graze.

Still Doc waited for Bart to mention Nebraska. But Bart could only look at Pirate and say, "Do you see that? A working cow horse that's raring to go."

They walked up to the blacksmith shop and sat in the doorway. The sun set and long shadows came and went beneath the ohia trees.

"The ranch hasn't changed," Doc said.

Bart walked over to the wall to show him the shoes, the little stack of failures, then on to the anvil. It was all there, the struggle of the past, as he outlined it to Doc.

"I couldn't have done it without you," he said and laughed. "When I got your last letter telling me to take it easy, it was there, right in English for me to follow."

"A letter doesn't teach you to make a horseshoe and fit it," Doc said, then stopped and waited, as though he wanted Bart to ask him some questions.

Bart could only talk of the ranch, the hills, their fun at the *luau*.

"They taught me to hula," he said, and got up to whistle a few bars and show Doc. "And, Doc"—he laughed—"I really fixed them on Santa Claus." He told about the airplane and the concert and the kids in the harmonica band.

Doc nodded. The hope he had died with his voice. He looked a long time at Bart, then at the long low buildings around them, and off to the hills.

"A harmonica band," he said. "That's great. Now maybe we'd better get my car and show up at the house."

"Sure." Bart was contrite. "Say hello to Tasy and Helen."

"Helen?" Doc's voice asked.

"Sure, Helen Hunter—oh," Bart broke off. "Well, they wouldn't have it any other way."

"Of course not," Doc said, and something seemed to settle in his voice. "Or course not," he added. "No other way."

They walked to get the car and brought it down to the house.

Bart got Doc's bag and they walked toward the door.

Helen Hunter came out to meet Doc and shook his hand, then suddenly, with a swift look at his face, gave him a kiss.

"Come in," she said. "Come in, Doc, and Bart." It was all she could say.

Chapter 23

WHERE IS HOME?

That evening after dinner Bart came in with a log to throw on the blaze. The kids were having another session of the harmonica band and there was Pirate to turn loose in the paddock, then he'd come in to hear Doc talk.

A big fire roared in the fireplace, and around it sat Helen and Tasy, Homer, Dick and Doc.

"Yes," Doc said. "I've been clear around the world and I'll probably have to go back to some of those places. There's a lot of hoof-and-mouth trouble that won't be cleared up in a minute." He paused and turned to Bart. "Well, Bart," he asked innocently. "Are you ready to go home?"

Bart rubbed a splinter from his hand as he tossed the stick on the fire, and his mind spun. Leave all this, the ranch, Helen and Dick who had been so wonderful, the kids who depended on him?

"Home? I am home," he blurted out, then reddened to the roots of his hair. What would the Hunters think, inviting himself to stay here? It sounded like disloyalty to Doc too, "I, I mean——" he added lamely as his voice trailed off.

But Doc smiled, and Dick looked at Helen, then at Doc, and finally to Bart.

At home enough to want to stay here, always?" Helen asked quietly. "And take the name of Hunter?"

Bart remembered his promise to Doc back there in the little animal hospital, that he'd never have any other name than Holiday. He reminded Doc of it now.

"Sure, Bart Holiday," Doc said, and rose to throw an arm around Bart's shoulders. "Bart Holiday Hunter."

In the silence they all waited.

Bart looked at Helen's face. It reminded him of the way she'd looked when he gave her the orchid. And at Dick's tight face, and at Doc's which wore a broad smile which didn't reach his eyes.

Bart took a handkerchief from his pocket. His hands were dirty. He wiped them and then had to blow his nose. The smoke from the fire must have gotten into his eyes. He wiped them.

"Bart Holiday Hunter," he said finally, and managed to smile. "Sounds wonderful to me."

Suddenly everybody was talking at once.

Doc said, "I hearby promote myself to uncle."

"Wonderful," Helen and Dick said almost in unison. "You can go to the University of Hawaii and be home summers," Helen said. "And we'll work on that grass problem," Dick added.

And Tasy kissed him between excited squeals.

Bart moved to the door. He had to get loose and straighten things out in his head.

"I'll be back in a little while," he said. "I promised to practice with the harmonica band."

They nodded and he let himself out of the door. For a moment he stood there on the stoop. From far up the paddock Pirate grazed in the moonlight. He could see him move along the mountain, effortlessly and with no limp.

As Bart walked along toward the hall, the big palomino recognized his step and sauntered down to throw his head over the fence.

Bart pulled his head down. The moonlight glimmered on the shoe, fit and trim.

From the hall came the sound of harmonicas playing "I'm an Old Cow Hand."

That was it. Suddenly everything smoothed out. Bart's hand tightened on Pirate's neck. "I've got to go, boy," he said. "See you later. See you plenty——"

The horse turned back to graze and Bart walked down the road singing softly, "I'm an old cow hand, from Hawaii land." He stopped at the door for a last look around, then nodded and moved to go in. "Yes, sir," he said, "yes, sir. That's it: just an old cow hand," and walked inside to start the practice with children who would grow up and be a working part of the Kukaiau along with him—and Pirate.